FROM THE NANCY DREW FILES

THE CASE: *When the curtain goes up on crime, Nancy is determined to bring down the culprit.*

CONTACT: *This could be the break Bess is waiting for . . . if Nancy can crack the case of her kidnapping.*

SUSPECTS: Zoe Adams—*The featured actress in the play, she's landed in the hospital, and she puts the blame on her replacement: Bess.*

Carlos Perez—*The director is concerned that the show may fold, but the publicity from a shooting and kidnapping could fill up the theater.*

Kate Grenoble—*Jordan's girlfriend thinks she should be the leading lady, and getting Zoe and Bess out of the way could get her the job.*

COMPLICATIONS: *Solving Bess's kidnapping could prove more difficult than Nancy imagined . . . especially when she gets kidnapped as well!*

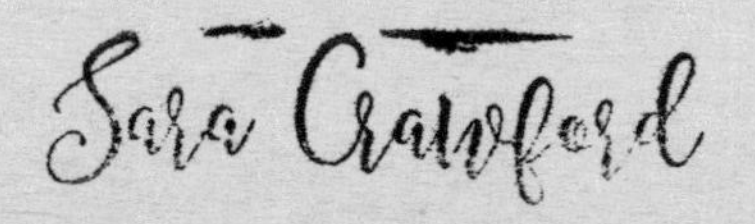

Books in The Nancy Drew Files® Series

#1 SECRETS CAN KILL
#2 DEADLY INTENT
#3 MURDER ON ICE
#4 SMILE AND SAY MURDER
#5 HIT AND RUN HOLIDAY
#6 WHITE WATER TERROR
#7 DEADLY DOUBLES
#8 TWO POINTS TO MURDER
#9 FALSE MOVES
#10 BURIED SECRETS
#11 HEART OF DANGER
#16 NEVER SAY DIE
#17 STAY TUNED FOR DANGER
#19 SISTERS IN CRIME
#31 TROUBLE IN TAHITI
#35 BAD MEDICINE
#36 OVER THE EDGE
#37 LAST DANCE
#41 SOMETHING TO HIDE
#43 FALSE IMPRESSIONS
#45 OUT OF BOUNDS
#46 WIN, PLACE OR DIE
#49 PORTRAIT IN CRIME
#50 DEEP SECRETS
#51 A MODEL CRIME
#53 TRAIL OF LIES
#54 COLD AS ICE
#55 DON'T LOOK TWICE
#56 MAKE NO MISTAKE
#57 INTO THIN AIR
#58 HOT PURSUIT
#59 HIGH RISK
#60 POISON PEN
#61 SWEET REVENGE
#62 EASY MARKS
#63 MIXED SIGNALS
#64 THE WRONG TRACK
#65 FINAL NOTES
#66 TALL, DARK AND DEADLY
#68 CROSSCURRENTS
#70 CUTTING EDGE
#71 HOT TRACKS
#72 SWISS SECRETS
#73 RENDEZVOUS IN ROME
#74 GREEK ODYSSEY
#75 A TALENT FOR MURDER
#76 THE PERFECT PLOT
#77 DANGER ON PARADE
#78 UPDATE ON CRIME
#79 NO LAUGHING MATTER
#80 POWER OF SUGGESTION
#81 MAKING WAVES
#82 DANGEROUS RELATIONS
#83 DIAMOND DECEIT
#84 CHOOSING SIDES
#85 SEA OF SUSPICION
#86 LET'S TALK TERROR
#87 MOVING TARGET
#88 FALSE PRETENSES
#89 DESIGNS IN CRIME
#90 STAGE FRIGHT
#91 IF LOOKS COULD KILL
#92 MY DEADLY VALENTINE
#93 HOTLINE TO DANGER
#94 ILLUSIONS OF EVIL
#95 AN INSTINCT FOR TROUBLE
#96 THE RUNAWAY BRIDE
#97 SQUEEZE PLAY
#98 ISLAND OF SECRETS
#99 THE CHEATING HEART
#100 DANCE TILL YOU DIE
#101 THE PICTURE OF GUILT
#102 COUNTERFEIT CHRISTMAS
#103 HEART OF ICE
#104 KISS AND TELL
#105 STOLEN AFFECTIONS
#106 FLYING TOO HIGH
#107 ANYTHING FOR LOVE
#108 CAPTIVE HEART
#109 LOVE NOTES
#110 HIDDEN MEANINGS
#111 THE STOLEN KISS
#112 FOR LOVE OR MONEY
#113 WICKED WAYS
#114 REHEARSING FOR ROMANCE

Available from ARCHWAY Paperbacks

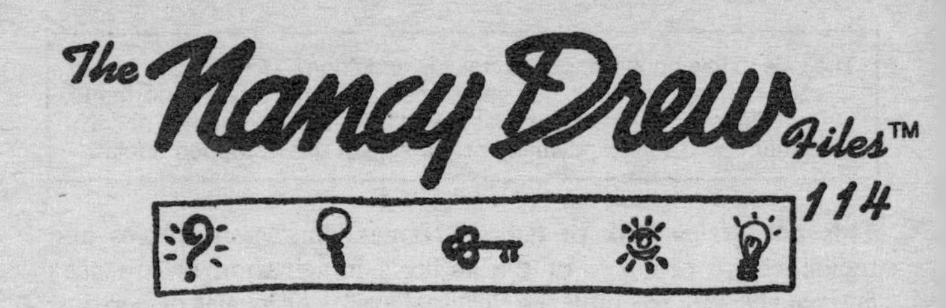

REHEARSING FOR ROMANCE

CAROLYN KEENE

AN ARCHWAY PAPERBACK
Published by POCKET BOOKS
New York London Toronto Sydney Tokyo Singapore

AN ARCHWAY PAPERBACK *Original*

An Archway Paperback published by
POCKET BOOKS, a division of Simon & Schuster Inc.
1230 Avenue of the Americas, New York, NY 10020

Produced by Mega-Books, Inc.

ISBN: 0-671-50355-3

First Archway Paperback printing April 1996

10 9 8 7 6 5 4 3 2 1

Printed in the U.S.A.

IL 6+

Chapter One

"I WOULDN'T MIND KISSING a handsome leading man," Nancy Drew admitted as she maneuvered her blue Mustang onto the highway. "But I couldn't do it in front of a whole audience."

"Well, I could," Nancy's friend Bess Marvin declared, "especially if the leading man happened to be a hunk like Jordan McCabe."

Nancy flashed Bess a quick grin, then eased the car into the fast lane.

"It's great that you're coming to watch the rehearsal, Nan," Bess went on. "I mean, *Mystery Loves Company* could be the hottest thing around. It was a huge Broadway hit and Carlos—he's our director—thinks it'll be a hit in Chicago, too. I'm so psyched about being in a thriller, even though I only play a small part—Hayley Karr, maid and amateur detective."

Nancy smoothed back her strawberry blond hair and laughed. "You're calling the role of an amateur detective a small part?"

Bess giggled. "Whoops. All I meant was, I don't have too many scenes."

"I'm sure you're going to add a lot to the role," Nancy told her friend in a more serious tone. "And besides—you're the understudy for the lead, too. That's a big deal."

"I guess so," Bess agreed. "But there's no way I'll ever get to take over for Zoe Adams. She'd go on if she were at death's door—acting is that important to her. You should have seen her at our first read-through. We were all reading from our scripts, but she already had her lines memorized."

"She sounds like a pro," Nancy said.

"She is—and she's used to getting what she wants. When she doesn't, watch out!"

Bess shook her head, then went on cheerfully. "You're right, though, Nance. I'm thrilled to have this part. I wish George could be here to see me."

George Fayne—Bess's cousin and Nancy's other best friend—was out of town participating in a track-and-field meet.

"We'll call her when we get home from Chicago," Nancy said. "After the rehearsal, we can grab a quick lunch and get back to River Heights late this afternoon."

"Sounds great," Bess agreed.

"By the way," Nancy said, "you still haven't told me the deal with Jordan McCabe. He's the star of that hot TV soap, *Heartbeats.* So why did he join the cast of *Mystery Loves Company*?"

"Jordan's trying really hard to prove he's a stage actor, too," Bess explained. "I think he's fantastic—really versatile."

"Well, I'm sure you'll impress him," Nancy said. "If you don't, it's his problem." She merged into the right lane, preparing to take the next exit.

"Thanks, Nan," Bess said. "When you meet him, you'll see exactly what I'm talking about—he's a hunk and a half!"

Nancy smiled to herself, mentally counting the number of times Bess had had crushes. Bess was almost as interested in romance as she was in theater.

Bess chattered away for the rest of the trip.

Nancy felt glad for her friend—landing a role in a professional theater production was a big break. And for Bess, a dream come true.

Nancy and Bess drove through downtown Chicago to the western edge of the Loop. When Nancy parked the Mustang outside the Remington Theater, it was 10:15—fifteen minutes before Bess's rehearsal was due to start.

"Great building!" Nancy exclaimed, admiring the broad marquee and ornate trim.

"It used to be a vaudeville theater," Bess told her. "Then it became a movie house. Now it's used for theater productions."

Bess slung her duffel bag over her shoulder. "Hi, Tim, hi, Hugh!" she called to two men standing in front of the theater. Nancy could see that they were mounting photos of the actors in one of the glass cases flanking the theater's entrance. A glamorous-looking head shot of Bess—showing off her pale blond hair and her pretty face—was among them.

"Tim Talcott is the theater's landlord—he's really got the acting bug, and he hangs out here when he's not selling property," Bess told Nancy as they approached.

Hearing her, Tim chuckled. He had long brown hair and a neatly trimmed beard. A cellular phone stuck out from one of his pockets. "I may be a businessman, but I'm an artist at heart," he told Nancy. "I love the theater—see as much as I can. I even like watching rehearsals. I'll see you girls later."

Bess turned to the taller man, who'd been standing beside Tim. Nancy guessed he was part of the crew, judging from his strong-looking build and clothes: blue jeans, work shirt, and work boots.

"Hugh, I'd like you to meet Nancy Drew. Nancy, this is Hugh Lundy. He's our stage manager. It's up to him to make all the technical elements of the play come together—the scenery changes, the sound, the lighting. He's got to know this theater inside and out."

"Sounds like a huge job," Nancy commented.

"I have lots of backup." Hugh shrugged. "We've got a bunch of college interns helping out and they're terrific."

"So are you," Bess offered.

The young man flushed as he ran his fingers through his blond hair. "Thanks, Bess," he said shyly.

Hmm, Nancy thought. Bess may have a crush on Jordan, but it looks like someone has a crush on her!

Nancy's hunch was confirmed a minute later when Bess looked around eagerly and asked if Jordan had arrived yet.

Hugh's face fell at the mention of the star's name. Before Hugh could answer, Bess whirled around and called out to another man hurrying past them. "Carlos, have you got a minute? I want you to meet a friend of mine."

Carlos appeared at Nancy's side.

"Nancy," Bess said, "meet the director of *Mystery Loves Company*—Carlos Perez. Carlos, Nancy Drew. She's the friend who's been helping me with my lines."

"Well, you're obviously a very good acting coach," Carlos said to Nancy. "Bess's performance just keeps getting better and better."

As Carlos grasped Nancy's hand warmly, she couldn't help noticing his striking features. Carlos had wavy black hair, velvety dark eyes, and smooth, olive skin. He wore a crisp white shirt with smooth-fitting black jeans.

Just then Hugh turned and began to walk away. Quickly, Carlos grabbed Hugh's arm. "Where do you think you're going?" he asked.

Hugh looked away for a second before he answered. "That new sofa is being delivered this morning, and I was just—"

"The sofa can wait," Carlos said firmly.

"Rehearsal starts in seven minutes, and I need you to check the hand props."

"Fine," Hugh said. He hurried off.

Nancy was a little startled by Carlos's sharp tone. Is he being harsh? she wondered. Or just taking charge of his crew?

"I'm glad you'll be in the audience today," Carlos said, turning back to Nancy. "I'd love to know what you think of the performance."

"I'll let you know," Nancy said. "But I warn you—I can be a tough critic."

"I think I'm up to the challenge," Carlos said, smiling broadly. "See you later."

As Carlos walked through the theater's entrance, Bess caught Nancy's arm. "He certainly noticed you, Nan." She giggled. "Maybe you could play a big role in his next production."

"No thanks, Bess," Nancy said with a laugh. "I'm not interested in an acting career."

Bess nodded. "I knew you'd say that. This may be Carlos's last production anyway."

Nancy was surprised to hear that. "What do you mean?"

Bess glanced at her watch and spoke quickly. "Carlos's last play was a flop. The critics loved it, but it never really took off. In the end, the production lost money. If *Mystery*

Loves Company doesn't fly, he could be painting sets instead of directing actors." Bess opened the front door and motioned for Nancy to go ahead of her.

"On stage, everyone!" came the call from backstage.

"I've got to run," said Bess. "I'll find you later."

Nancy walked through the lobby and into the theater's auditorium. She admired the intricately carved balconies, the proscenium stage, and the plush red seats. Nancy noticed Carlos sitting in the center of the house. With a legal pad and pen in hand, he was poised to take notes during the rehearsal.

Nancy sat closer to the stage, settling herself one seat away from a young woman with shoulder-length auburn hair. When Nancy introduced herself, she was greeted with a limp handshake.

"I'm Kate Grenoble," the woman said haughtily.

With her flawless skin and elegant features, Kate struck Nancy as being an actress. "Friend of the director's?" Nancy asked.

"Friend of Jordan's," the other woman said pointedly, keeping her eyes focused on the stage.

Nancy followed Kate's gaze. The actors were assembling onstage. Jordan McCabe stood to one side, looking calm and composed—and even more handsome than Nancy had remembered from *Heartbeats.* No wonder Bess was excited about working with him.

"We're going to do a complete run-through today," Carlos called from his seat. "If you mess up a line, just keep going. I'll be timing the run-through, focusing on pacing to make sure there are no slow spots. Ready? Act one, scene one."

Nancy took in the lush-looking set—a drawing room paneled in dark wood. At center stage were twin love seats upholstered in green crushed velvet. An enormous framed portrait of a man dominated the wide fireplace mantel against the back wall.

The play opened with Jordan McCabe reading the paper while Bess dusted the room around him. Nancy was pleased to see that the gestures she had helped Bess work out were smooth and natural-looking on stage. And her dialogue with Jordan moved along nicely.

When Zoe Adams made her entrance a few minutes later, Nancy immediately felt the leading lady's presence. Zoe was statuesque—nearly six feet tall. Her thick raven-colored hair fell to her waist, contrasting with her white dress. Entranced, Nancy watched the scene unfold.

"Xena! What are you doing in town?" Jordan said indignantly.

"I was passing through on my way to Eden Prairie," Zoe answered. "Aren't you glad to see me?"

"Of course." Jordan arched his eyebrows. "What man wouldn't be glad to see his ex-wife?"

Nancy chuckled. Jordan had a good sense of comic timing, and he seemed equally at ease in the play's more serious moments. A quick glance to her left let Nancy know that the other woman was also rapt; Kate seemed to hang on every word that Jordan spoke.

On the stage, Zoe arranged herself on a love seat. "Remember how happy we once were?" she said. "I would read down here while you were upstairs working. Whenever I got lonely, I would take the broom and tap out our special signal. Then you'd come down to keep me company." Zoe grasped a broom that Bess had left in the corner and tapped a few times on the alcove ceiling.

"I remember as if it were yesterday," Jordan said, moving closer.

As the play progressed, Nancy pieced together the story: Zoe arrives in town, hoping for a reunion with Jordan, her ex-husband. But the local woman Jordan had recently been seeing has just been found murdered, and Zoe becomes the prime suspect in the investigation. The evidence against Zoe mounts, but the real culprit turns out to be Jordan himself: He killed his girlfriend because she was trying to blackmail him, having discovered a secret about his past. When Zoe learns the truth, Jordan tries to get rid of her, too.

Before Nancy knew it, the play was close to its final moments. The two characters edged toward each other on the love seat and embraced. Jordan leaned into Zoe, and the sultry leading lady prepared to be kissed.

Suddenly Nancy heard Kate stir in her seat. The young woman, rattling her shopping bags, got up noisily. Then she pushed past Nancy and marched up the aisle. When she reached the exit, she turned back for a moment to glare at the actors on the stage. As she walked out, she let the auditorium door slam behind her.

On the stage Zoe was stock-still, Jordan's hand on her shoulder.

"What's wrong—why are you stopping?" Carlos's voice rose from his seat.

"How am I supposed to concentrate with all that noise?" Zoe said, pulling away from Jordan and crossing her arms angrily.

"It was a little distracting," Jordan said calmly. "But why don't we just go on?"

Zoe ignored him. "Carlos!" she demanded. "Why can't you keep that woman out of here? Every time she shows up she causes trouble."

"I thought you liked an audience," Carlos said with a chuckle. His mild joke was obviously an attempt to lighten the mood, but it had the opposite effect.

"I don't want anyone—especially some overpaid soap star—to interrupt me." Zoe rose from her seat and began to pace the stage.

Jordan stood up as well. "Hold on a second. I apologize for Kate—okay? Now, can we please just finish this play?"

Zoe whirled toward him. "You'd rather be doing this scene with her, wouldn't you?" She spat out the words at Jordan. "Is that why she comes to every rehearsal? To learn *my* lines?" Zoe crossed the stage to the hearth and stood in front of the fake fire.

"Well," Jordan said, losing control of his temper, "at least she knows how to play a love scene."

Even from her seat in the audience, Nancy

could see the sparks flash in Zoe's eyes. The actress suddenly turned and grabbed a ceramic vase from the mantel. "I finally know what you think about me, Jordan. Now let me show you how I feel about you."

Then, in one fluid motion, Zoe hurled the heavy vase—directly at Jordan's head!

Chapter Two

FOR A SPLIT SECOND, Jordan stood paralyzed. Then he threw himself down, dodging the heavy vase in the nick of time. It smashed against the wall behind him.

Before anyone onstage could move, Nancy jumped from her seat and leaped up to the stage. She pulled Jordan to his feet. "That was a close call," she said. "Are you all right?"

"I'm fine." He breathed heavily, glaring at Zoe. The leading lady folded her arms across her chest, apparently satisfied with her gesture.

"Jordan!" Bess had been watching the scene from the wings and now ran onstage, followed by several other members of the cast and crew.

Zoe pushed her way past everyone and strode into the wings.

Jordan watched her go. "She's incredible," he murmured. "She's not even going to apologize."

"You okay, Jordan?" Carlos called out as he jogged up the steps. When the TV star nodded, Carlos made a meek joke. "I'd like to see that kind of emotion *in* the play.

Nancy smiled. Carlos sure seemed to know how to defuse a tense situation.

"Let's try to forget about this for now," he called to the cast. Take a half hour, everyone. I'll see you all back here at one sharp. Okay?"

A murmur of assent went through the cast members. As the crowd dispersed, Nancy overheard a few comments. Apparently, this was not Zoe's first tantrum. Everyone seemed fed up with her behavior.

Nancy put her arm around Bess. "Let's go get some coffee—my treat. We'll go to that terrific-looking café next door."

"It's a deal," Bess said.

"I'll join you," Carlos said. "I need a moment of sanity."

Nancy noticed Hugh sweeping up the pieces of the broken vase. At Carlos's words, he looked up.

"We're just going next door for coffee—how about coming with us?" Nancy said to Hugh.

"He can't," Carlos cut in. "He's got too much to attend to here." To Hugh, he added, "I don't see how you could afford to spend any time with us—not with all the trouble we've been having lately."

"I don't know what you're talking about," Hugh answered in a low voice.

"Are you forgetting about the ruined costumes? And how about the collapsing love seat? This is supposed to be a drama we're putting on here, not a comedy of errors."

"None of that was my fault," Hugh said quickly.

"Fine." Carlos's tone was chilly. "I still advise you to stay here and make sure there are no more problems." He turned abruptly and escorted the girls to the front of the theater.

Nancy gave Bess a quizzical look; Bess answered with a shrug. The tension in the air was unmistakable. Nancy resolved to find out as much as she could during their coffee break with Carlos.

Rick's Café was bustling, with every indoor table filled.

"How about dining alfresco?" Carlos suggested.

"That'd be great," Nancy said, following Carlos outside to a round table with a red- and white-striped umbrella.

"Don't you just love all this?" Bess said after they had ordered iced cappuccinos.

"All what?" Carlos asked. He doodled distractedly on the restaurant's paper tablecloth.

"This neighborhood," Bess went on. "It's just so cool. I wish we had some time to shop—the boutique across the street looks great."

Nancy turned to see the trendy clothes and shoes in the store window facing them.

"It wasn't always this hip," Carlos began. "When we first moved in—"

"Carlos!" A stocky, square-jawed man clapped the director on the back.

"Hey, Rick." Carlos smiled and introduced the girls to the restaurant's owner. "Looks like business is booming," Carlos observed.

"Can't complain," Rick said. "We'll soon be bursting at the seams. Expecting a crowd of your own on Friday?"

"I hope so," Carlos answered uncertainly.

After Rick had moved to another table,

Nancy turned to Carlos. "You sounded worried about the show."

"I am," Carlos confirmed. "We open Friday, and if we don't make this play a hit . . ." His voice drifted off. Abruptly, he leaned closer to Nancy and Bess, and confided, "Between the three of us, *Mystery Loves Company* is a last-ditch effort. The company's funding runs out with this play."

"I can see why you'd be anxious," Nancy said sympathetically. "That sounds like a lot of pressure."

"My father has put more money into this company than you could imagine," Carlos lamented, "and the well's dry now."

"Is he your major benefactor?" Nancy asked.

"He and Stella—Stella Brentman. She's a patron and also our publicist—I'm sure you'll meet her before the week's over. She and my father became partners in the deal three and a half years ago."

"Who is your father?" Bess asked. "Have I met him?"

Carlos shook his head. "He lives in Spain—I grew up in the States, but five years ago my mother died, and my father wanted to return to Spain, to go back to the culture that he came from. If I blow this, I'll be so ashamed. . . ."

"It's going to be a hit," Bess reassured him. "I mean, who *wouldn't* buy a ticket to see Jordan McCabe?"

"At this point, ticket sales are only part of my worries," Carlos said. He looked at Bess. "From the very beginning, I've had trouble with the cast *and* the crew, especially Hugh. He seems to attract mishaps. He 'accidentally' let costumes get damaged by the sprinkler system. And though he's supposed to check out every hand and set prop, the bottom fell out of the love seat the first time Jordan sat on it. We're lucky Jordan was such a good sport about it. He refers to it as the killer couch now."

Carlos sighed. "Sometimes I think Hugh is trying to get revenge on me," he concluded.

"What do you mean?" asked Nancy. Her curiosity was really piqued now.

"Hugh's a budding playwright. He gave me a script to read a few months ago, and I think he's angry because I wouldn't produce it. It has promise, but at this point I can't afford to produce the work of an unknown." Carlos threw up his hands. "Anyway, I can't get rid of

Hugh. It's too late in the game to hire a new stage manager."

"Have you talked to him about the accidents?" asked Nancy.

Carlos nodded. "Of course. He claims that he doesn't know what happened, and I can't exactly prove that either accident was his fault." Carlos paused. "He used to do a terrific job. I don't know what's gotten into him lately. . . ."

"Zoe seems a little difficult, too," Nancy observed. "Is that what you meant about cast problems?"

"Zoe's been one big headache," Carlos confirmed. "She's so temperamental—you saw a fine example of that today."

"That's for sure," Bess agreed.

"It sounds like you've got your hands full," Nancy commented.

"On top of everything, Jordan's been tough to deal with as well," Carlos went on. "He really pushed for Kate to play opposite him—she's his girlfriend, you know."

Nancy glanced at Bess and saw her eyes cloud for a second. Maybe in her eagerness to do a good job and get Jordan's attention, Bess hadn't paid much attention to the fact that Jordan had a girlfriend.

"The whole situation sounds pretty complicated," Nancy said. "I guess that explains why Kate got huffy during the love scene."

"If Kate is Jordan's girlfriend—and an actress," Bess said slowly, "then why did Zoe get the role?"

"Star power," Carlos responded. "Zoe Adams is a known quantity—and a bigger name—especially on the stage. Besides, she was raised here in Chicago and—well, you know how fans are—they go crazy for local talent. I knew she was more of a draw than Kate, and at this point every ticket counts. Besides, Kate doesn't have much stage experience."

"It sounds like you made the right decision," Nancy reassured him.

"I know I did," Carlos said. "The funny thing is, Zoe would like to trade places with Kate almost as much as Kate wants to trade places with Zoe. She's been trying to break into the soaps for years—the money is much better in television, and I understand Zoe's pretty broke these days." He shook his head.

Nancy found herself feeling sorry for him. This guy is really stressed, she thought, and I can see why.

Carlos glanced at his watch, then got to his

feet. "I'd better head back to the theater," he said. "Who knows what havoc Hugh might have wreaked in the last half hour." He reached into his jeans pocket and took out his wallet. He paused and turned to Nancy.

"Do you mind if I tell you that you're a good listener?" he asked quietly. "You, too, Bess," he added. He put down a few bills on the table. "I think this should cover my cappuccino. See you both in a few minutes."

When Carlos had gone, Bess let out a sigh. "So Jordan and Kate are tighter than I thought." She gave Nancy a smile. "I guess the good news is that Carlos really likes you. I wish Jordan liked me half as much!"

Nancy smiled at her friend's generous nature. "At least we know the score with Jordan and Kate. And, who knows, maybe he'll get tired of her at some point and you'll get together with him." Nancy tried to sound hopeful, but privately she didn't think Bess stood a chance. As TV stars, Jordan and Kate were both part of another world.

On the way back to the theater, Bess walked quickly. Nancy sensed that even though Bess now knew Jordan was taken, she was still eager to see him. Bess bounded up the steps leading to the stage door, grabbing hold of the ornate iron banister.

The next thing Nancy heard was Bess shrieking, "Oh, no!" Nancy looked up and saw, to her horror, that Bess had lost her balance. The metal banister had given way, and before Nancy could do anything, Bess had tumbled down nearly a dozen steps.

Nancy rushed toward her friend, but someone else reached her first. Hugh dashed down the steps from the stage door to Bess's side. He slipped his arm around her waist and helped her to her feet.

"I—I think I'm okay," Bess said tentatively. "I mean, I feel a little ridiculous, but—what exactly happened?"

Nancy let Hugh tend to Bess as she examined the broken banister. At the end of the long metal bar, she noticed a pair of holes, apparently for screws. She scanned the steps and the sidewalk below for the missing fasteners but could find only one. The ornate wrought-iron banister certainly looked old—and original to the building.

"I don't understand what happened," Nancy heard Hugh saying. "I told my crew to check all the entrances the day the production started rehearsal. You could have gotten really hurt, Bess," he added, sounding concerned.

"I'm fine—a few scrapes and bruises, but nothing serious," Bess said lightly. "Thanks, Hugh, see you later." She dusted herself off and rushed into the building's main entrance.

Nancy watched Hugh's expression carefully. As Bess disappeared, the corners of his mouth turned down and his gaze lingered on the door for a moment or two.

"What do you think happened out here?" Nancy asked him.

"Who knows?" Hugh said. "I'm supposed to be responsible for the set—but not keeping this old theater standing," he said bitterly. "Carlos acts like it's my fault the building's falling apart. He has a problem with everything I do—nothing's good enough for him!"

These two guys are really in a tangle, Nancy thought. "Why do you think Carlos is so rough on you?" she asked.

Hugh bit a fingernail, then opened the stage door abruptly. "Carlos is just picking on me because he can't pick on any of his prima donna actresses—Bess excluded," he said angrily.

Nancy followed him into the theater, staying close as he walked backstage.

"I'm not having much fun at all on this production," Hugh admitted. "But somehow I feel like I need to stick around." Nancy nodded, wondering if it was his feelings for Bess that kept him at the Remington Theater.

"I know what you mean," Nancy told him. "I think Bess—" But before she could finish her thought, a cry rose from behind the curtain.

"FIRE!" came the shout. It was Jordan's booming voice.

Is the cast rehearsing a scene I don't remember? Nancy wondered as she spun around. Instead, clouds of smoke—real smoke—were billowing across the stage. Nancy gasped as the entire cast and crew ran backstage and raced for the door!

Chapter Three

NANCY RUSHED OUT of the theater with everyone else. "Did someone call the fire department?" she asked Bess.

"I'm not sure," Bess admitted. "I know Tim ran for a fire extinguisher."

After a few minutes of waiting with the panicked cast and crew, Nancy's curiosity got the better of her. "Cover for me," she whispered to Bess. "I'm going back to take a look."

"Just be careful, Nan," Bess warned.

Back inside the theater, Nancy walked quickly toward the rear of the house. There were no flames to be seen, but the smell of smoke was strong.

An electrical fire? Nancy wondered. She

followed her nose to the last row of seats. There she found an opening in the floor, with a ladder leading down. She leaned in and saw Tim Talcott, fire extinguisher in hand, spraying a large black box.

"Looks like you've licked it," Nancy said. She climbed down the ladder.

"Oh, Nancy." Tim sounded surprised. "Yeah, no problem, though it could've turned out to be another Chicago Fire." He pointed to the scorched cable on the dimmer box that housed a tangle of wires.

Just then Carlos appeared, followed closely by Hugh.

"I can't believe this!" the director exploded. "*Another* accident?" He turned to Hugh. "Your carelessness is going to cost us this play!"

"Hold on now," Tim intervened. "I don't think this is Hugh's fault. This place just can't handle a lot of electrical power."

Nancy saw Hugh breathe a sigh of relief.

"But Hugh installed extra circuits and new wiring last month," Carlos said angrily. "That was supposed to solve our problem."

"Even with the new setup," Tim responded calmly, "there's no way you can expect this place to be trouble free. It's too old for that—

it was built in 1879. I hate to say it, but what you really need is a better-equipped space—a more modern theater."

Carlos shook his head vehemently. "I love this place. And I can't even think about moving the play so far along into production." He turned to Hugh. "I'm really disappointed that you would do a shoddy job."

"I didn't do a shoddy job at all," Hugh protested. "With the new wiring, I'm positive we had enough juice to support the extra lights."

Nancy examined the charred area. She said matter-of-factly, "It's not likely that the additional power itself caused the fire. If the system was maxed out, the circuit breaker would've tripped automatically—so there wouldn't have been a fire." She shook her head. "It looks like something—or someone—else caused this fire."

Carlos ran his fingers through his hair.

Nancy watched him closely. She wasn't sure how many more incidents the stressed-out director could handle today.

As if he were reading Nancy's thoughts, Carlos exclaimed, "This is the last straw! No more for this afternoon. We'll try rehearsal again this evening at six sharp." Then he muttered under his breath, "And maybe we'll actually get through it this time."

"Quite a dramatic day, wouldn't you say?" Nancy asked as she and Bess drove back to River Heights later that night. The cast had managed to get another rehearsal in, and things had gone more smoothly. Still, Nancy found herself mentally going over the accidents in the old theater.

"Uh-huh." Bess sounded dejected.

"He's not the only guy out there, you know," Nancy said, guessing the source of her friend's dark mood.

Bess was silent.

"Have you noticed how good-looking Hugh is?" Nancy ventured.

"Nice try, Nan," Bess responded. "But Jordan's *it* for me. I can't look at anyone else right now—even though Hugh's a sweetheart. He always seems to be there when I need help."

"I wish I could cheer you up somehow," said Nancy.

"Believe me," Bess told her, "I'm totally relieved that you were there when I found out about Jordan and Kate." She added, "It'd be great if you could come to rehearsal every day until we open."

"I think I should," Nancy told her friend. "That fire seemed sort of suspicious. I'd like to find out how the fire started."

Bess nodded. "It does seem as if something funny is going on. Do you think someone is actually trying to sabotage the play?"

"Maybe," Nancy said. "There's only one way to find out, and that's my investigating."

She pulled into Bess's driveway. "It might be better not to tell anyone I'm a detective, though. If I work undercover, I can probably get more answers."

"Sounds good," Bess said, as she hopped out of the Mustang. "See you in the morning."

"Nine o'clock?" Nancy called.

"Ugh" was Bess's only reply.

Nancy awoke before her alarm clock sounded. She checked the time—7:32. Nancy rose and opened the window to check the weather. It was another perfect spring day: warm with a slight breeze.

After showering and blow-drying her hair, Nancy went to her closet to choose an outfit for the day. She thought of the two hours she and Bess would be spending in the car—definitely something comfortable, she concluded, but nice. She finally chose a long, flowered, gauzy skirt that fluttered around her ankles and a white wrap top.

Less than three hours later, Nancy was sitting in the audience watching the run-through. Zoe had turned up for rehearsal as if nothing had happened the day before. Nancy had noticed that Jordan was businesslike onstage, trying not to antagonize Zoe. And, fortunately, Kate was nowhere to be seen.

Nancy was soon immersed in the action of the play. Time passed quickly, and before she knew it, the climax was at hand.

A dark figure clad in a black cat-burglar costume strode onto the stage and approached Zoe. Nancy marveled at how threatening Jordan looked in his costume. He moved toward Zoe, and she stepped back to avoid him.

"Give me the letter!" Jordan demanded.

"Never! This letter is the only evidence against you. And anyway, why should I?" Zoe challenged.

"Because you love me," Jordan said.

"Not good enough. Try again," Zoe countered.

Jordan brandished a revolver. "How about this for a reason?" he countered.

"As if you had the courage," Zoe said huskily.

"I'll prove it to you," Jordan said, aiming the weapon at the portrait on the wall beside Zoe.

The gunshot rang out, and Nancy shuddered, though she knew the revolver was loaded with blanks.

A strangled cry rose from the stage. Nancy watched as Zoe staggered forward, sinking to her knees. Wow! Nancy thought. Zoe Adams might be difficult, but she can really act.

But as Nancy stared at the stage, where Zoe Adams was kneeling doubled over, a pool of blood was forming around the actress.

The pearl-handled revolver had been loaded with real bullets, Nancy realized, not blanks. Zoe Adams had been shot!

Chapter Four

FOR A MOMENT Jordan remained in character, looking at Zoe coolly. Then, all at once, he seemed to realize what had happened.

"Call an ambulance!" Jordan shouted. Actors and crew members quickly clustered around the leading lady. Carlos raced to the stage and pushed his way through the crowd, then crouched next to Zoe.

Nancy leaped out of her seat and fled past the rows of empty seats. In the lobby, she grasped the receiver of the pay phone and punched 911, calmly and swiftly giving the theater's address to the emergency operator. When she uttered the words "gunshot wound," she felt the tiny hairs on her arms stand on end. She couldn't believe the shooting had really occurred.

After reporting the accident, she returned to the group gathered around Zoe. The leading lady had been carefully covered with a blanket. By now, she was weeping uncontrollably.

"I had no idea the thing was loaded," Jordan said to no one in particular. Nancy scanned his expression. The actor seemed genuinely upset, but it was impossible to tell for sure.

"Where was she hit?" Nancy asked him.

"It's her right arm," he said, choking on the words.

Nancy could see that someone had already made a tourniquet to stem the bleeding. It appeared to be more than a flesh wound, though how serious, Nancy couldn't tell.

Bess appeared, still in her floor-length dressing gown. "I can't believe it," she whispered. Nancy noticed that the color had drained from Bess's face. She touched her friend's shoulder.

"We've got to get to the bottom of this," Nancy said urgently. "The banister breaking—and even the fire—could have been accidents. But blanks don't get replaced by live ammunition accidentally. Somebody must be out to sabotage this production—or worse."

"Now I'm really glad you're here, Nan."

Nancy heard the tremor in Bess's voice. She was about to comfort her friend when she was interrupted by Carlos. The director had noticed Hugh standing at the edge of the circle around Zoe. "You're fired!" Carlos bellowed.

Hugh looked shocked, but Carlos didn't give him time to answer. "That gun was your responsibility!" Carlos shouted. "She could have died. Do you realize that?"

"Yes, I realize that," Hugh said. "And I'm telling you I put blanks in that revolver. If you didn't have it in for me already, you'd believe that."

"Give me your keys," Carlos demanded.

"What keys?" Hugh asked, startled.

"To the front door, the back door, and all the backstage rooms. I want all of them *now,"* the director commanded.

Hugh's gaze shifted from Carlos to Bess, and then to Nancy. "I—I don't know where they are," he stammered. "I must have left them somewhere."

Everyone was silent, except Zoe, who moaned in pain. Jordan patted her cheek, reassuring her that the ambulance would arrive shortly.

As if on cue, the sirens sounded and the

ambulance screeched to a halt outside the double glass doors. Just behind was a police car, and Nancy knew the questioning would soon begin.

"You'd better find those keys fast," she heard Carlos tell Hugh, "and drop them off in my office by nine A.M. tomorrow. Got it? Stick around now, though. I'm sure the police want to talk to you."

Five minutes later two police officers questioned Carlos while the rest of the cast and crew waited nervously onstage. Nancy stood next to Bess, just inches from the spot where the actress had been wounded.

With the stage lights up, Nancy felt as if she had stepped into the drama she had just seen enacted. It was an eerie feeling—with Jordan shooting Zoe, real life had begun to parallel the play.

Officer Streithorst, the policeman in charge, turned to Jordan. "How much ammunition was in the gun?" he asked.

"I couldn't answer that—I'm not the one responsible for props," he said evenly, looking straight at Hugh.

"Who loaded the gun?" the officer asked Jordan.

"I did," Hugh said miserably. "I put in one

full round of blanks." He added more forcefully, "And I'm sure they were blanks."

"Do you have the box?" the officer asked.

"I had it until this morning, when the trash was picked up," Hugh said.

Carlos returned to his seat in time to interject, "Convenient."

Officer Streithorst was quiet for a moment. "I want you all to know that this investigation will continue—and I may have more questions for some of you. One more thing"—he turned to Carlos—"how long has this production been in rehearsal?"

"Three weeks," Carlos told him.

Suddenly, there was a commotion at the far end of the theater. The main doors flew open, and a group of people streamed down the two main aisles. The group included several photographers, who pointed their cameras at the stage.

"Mr. Perez!" a woman shouted. "Is it true your leading man was murdered this morning?" The reporter hopped onto the stage.

"Not quite," Carlos said. "Our leading lady, Zoe Adams, received a minor wound. She is being taken to the hospital now." Carlos's voice sounded calm, but he looked dazed, Nancy noted.

Hugh had already fled from the reporters and was standing at the far end of the stage. Strobes flashed and questions flew. Nancy saw one reporter whip out a laptop computer from her shoulder bag and begin typing as she fired questions at cast members.

Nancy turned to see that Tim had arrived and was holding court with a gaggle of reporters.

"This neighborhood has changed enormously in the past year," he was saying. "And the Remington's going to be in the center of it all. You see new businesses moving into this neighborhood every day: restaurants, boutiques—you name it."

One reporter closed his notepad and moved on. Nancy didn't blame him. Tim sounded more like an actor doing a commercial for the neighborhood than a landlord answering questions about the safety of his building.

Just when the action seemed about to die down, a tall thin woman trailing a white chiffon scarf flew down the aisle. She mounted the stage and said loudly, as if playing to an audience, "Carlos! I'm so sorry!" She kissed the director European-style, on both cheeks.

Carlos drew back. "Nancy Drew, meet Stella Brentman, one of this theater's most important patrons and our publicist." Nancy shook the woman's hand, which was cool to the touch.

Stella began speaking softly to Carlos. Nancy strained to hear every word. "When you called and told me about the fire, I thought I'd alert the media for a bit of publicity. But now—a real shooting! This is more than we could have dreamed of."

Nancy was shocked by Stella's attitude. She actually seemed pleased about the shooting. Then again, Nancy reasoned, maybe the publicist was just doing her job—generating publicity for the show.

Nancy watched Stella work the crowd. Stella seemed determined to have the reporters speak to every member of the cast, especially Jordan McCabe.

Disgusted, Nancy turned away. Stella Brentman's behavior only made her more determined to figure out what was going on at the Remington Theater. Publicity was one thing, but people getting injured was a serious matter.

The police officers were dusting the gun for fingerprints, but Nancy knew it wasn't likely to lead to anything: Jordan had been wearing gloves during the scene, so any fingerprints on the gun had probably been erased. There had to be other clues around.

Several minutes later Carlos escorted Stella and the last of the journalists out of the theater. Then he stood center-stage, clapped his hands, and called the cast together. Everyone looked exhausted from the ordeal.

"I know you're all shaken up—I am, too," Carlos confessed. "But with or without Zoe the show must go on." He took a deep breath. "And that means Bess will be taking over the role of Xena."

Bess gasped, clasping her hand over her mouth. Nancy imagined her friend had mixed feelings. As much as Bess had wanted the lead, Nancy was sure she would rather have gotten it in a different way.

Bess took a deep breath. "I'll be glad to help. I can do it—I have all the lines memorized," she said softly.

"Fine. Now we just need to fill the role of the maid," Carlos said, walking to the edge of the stage. "Ms. Drew," he said formally, "your services are required onstage."

"W-what do you mean?" Nancy's heart began to pound.

"Come on up—I'll tell you all about it." Reluctantly, Nancy followed the director's lead. She had a feeling she knew what was coming. She mounted the steps and sat on a folding chair next to Bess, who looked at Nancy excitedly.

"Nancy Drew will be taking over the role of the maid," Carlos announced.

"But I'm not an actress," Nancy protested.

"Ah," Carlos countered. "You are better than a professional in this case. You helped Bess learn the part, so you already know it. And you've been watching the rehearsals. Besides, this is an emergency—our understudy has no understudy."

If only he weren't so charming *and* logical, Nancy thought, sighing. She didn't want to abandon her detective role. But, she had to admit, becoming part of the cast might make it easier to find out who had put the bullets in the gun.

" 'Yes' is the only word I can hear," Carlos declared. "For now," he went on, "we'll rehearse only the scenes with Nancy and Bess. Then tonight at eight we'll do a full dress rehearsal of the play. Places, everyone."

"I can't believe it," Bess whispered to Nancy before taking her place. "This was not what I meant when I said I wanted the lead."

"I know," Nancy said. "Maybe you can think of it as a way of helping Carlos."

In spite of her discomfort about her new role, Bess's blue eyes twinkled for a second. "At least I'll get to kiss Jordan!"

Within minutes the actors had reconvened onstage. Carlos began rehearsing the opening scenes with Nancy, Bess, and Jordan.

"Oh, my—I suppose no one has told you yet." Nancy heard her voice as she dusted the drawing-room table. "Catherine Daniels was found murdered half an hour ago." Nancy's stage fright faded as the scene went on. All the coaching she'd done with Bess *had* helped. To her surprise, she really did know the lines. At Bess's first cue, Nancy scurried offstage.

As she walked into the wings, Nancy was surprised to see Hugh. She had expected him to be gone from the theater. She moved next to him and saw that his attention was riveted on Bess's performance.

"Remember how happy we once were?" Bess was saying. "I would read down here while you were upstairs working. Whenever I got lonely, I would take the broom and tap out our special signal on the alcove ceiling. Then you'd come down to keep me company." Just as Zoe had done, Bess retrieved the broom and rapped on the alcove ceiling.

"How are you doing?" Nancy asked.

"Not well." Hugh shook his head. "Let's put it this way. I'd like to tap out an SOS signal. Nobody believes me—not Carlos or the police. On top of that, I'm out of a job. I need help—big time."

Nancy studied his face. He certainly looked shaken by the morning's events. But Nancy couldn't be sure about him. According to Carlos, he had a very good motive for sabotaging the production.

Be careful, she cautioned herself. This guy might be a master playwright, following his own script.

Nancy turned her attention back to the stage. Jordan moved closer to Bess on the couch and leaned over to kiss her. Nancy craned her neck to watch her friend's big moment. From where Nancy stood, the electricity between the two actors felt real.

"Wow!" Bess breathed.

"I don't believe that line is in the script," Hugh said dryly.

"That's it! I've seen enough already!" It was Kate's voice.

Nancy peered around the edge of the curtain to see into the audience. Jordan's girlfriend was coming down the aisle, red-faced and furious.

Onstage, Bess and Jordan broke apart.

"Bess Marvin!" Kate shouted in a threatening tone. "The part of Xena belongs to me—not some amateur like you."

Nancy glanced back at her friend, whose face had grown pale under the spotlights. "But . . ." Bess began to sputter. "Carlos asked me—"

Kate sliced into her words with the swiftness of a carving knife. "I am prepared to do whatever it takes to get the part," she said, her dark eyes smoldering. "So you'd better watch out."

Chapter Five

A SHOCKED SILENCE followed Kate's warning. Then the TV actress turned on her heel and charged back up the aisle. Jordan jumped off the stage and dashed after her.

"Hold it!" Carlos commanded. Jordan kept moving. "I've got to talk to her," he shouted over his shoulder.

In a flash, Carlos was beside Jordan, his arm around him in a fatherly way. "We both know she didn't mean a word of that speech," Carlos said. "Right now, we need you here. You'll have time later to speak with her."

"But—" Jordan said.

"We open tomorrow," Carlos said imploringly. "You and Bess are going to look awfully foolish if you don't have your act together."

Good tactic, Nancy thought. Carlos was appealing to the actor's sense of vanity. After all, Jordan had a lot at stake—his reputation as a stage actor.

"I guess you're right," Jordan relented, reluctantly mounting the stage once again.

Nancy walked quietly out to the stage steps, where Bess stood watching the actor and director negotiate.

"Do you think she meant it, Nan? Will I be sorry I ever got involved in this whole thing?" Bess whispered.

Nancy saw tears in her friend's eyes.

"I hope not," Nancy answered truthfully. "I think Kate is just trying to throw you." Nancy pulled a tissue from her pocket and gave it to Bess, who wiped her eyes. "Anyway, you'll be fine with me around," she reassured her friend.

Inside she was fighting a moment of doubt. Just how far would Kate go to get the lead? Was Bess in any kind of real danger?

Jordan joined the girls. "Are you okay?" he asked his costar gently.

Bess nodded. "I'm just a little nervous," she

confided. Jordan placed his arm around her shoulders.

"You know," he began, "Kate's just blowing off steam—she does it all the time. It really stresses me out, too." He grinned. "I mean, it's part of my job. I've *got* to do love scenes with beautiful women!"

Bess blushed. Nancy could see that her friend was encouraged. She only hoped it was in the right way.

For the next two hours, Carlos worked with Nancy and Bess on their scenes. His manner was calm and reassuring; Nancy felt grateful for his direction.

Finally, they came to the moment of the gunshot. Although the police had impounded the weapon and Jordan was only using his finger, Nancy still tensed.

"As if you had the courage," Bess said.

"I'll prove it to you," Jordan answered, aiming his finger at the picture on the wall.

"Bang," he said. Nancy felt all her muscles relax. The actors finished the scene. Carlos called the five o'clock dinner break.

"Thanks, Jordan," Bess murmured. "C'mon, Nan." Bess touched Nancy's elbow.

"You were both great," Nancy heard behind her. She turned to see Carlos approaching.

"I rushed my lines," Nancy said, shaking her head. She wouldn't let herself be too susceptible to Carlos's flattery. At this point, she had no idea who was behind the accidents, and she resolved to be wary of everyone—including the director.

"How's Zoe doing?" Nancy asked, changing the subject.

"Better than I thought," Carlos responded. "I'm going to run out and see her now. Will you join me?" he asked. "Zoe would probably like the company."

"Be happy to," Nancy said.

Perfect, she thought. It would give her a chance to see Zoe and ask some questions. "As long as it's okay with Bess," Nancy added, looking at her friend.

"Sure," Bess replied.

Carlos nodded. "I have a few errands to do first. I'll meet you there."

A few minutes later, as they drove to the hospital, Bess asked, "Do you think he really meant it?"

"Who meant what?" asked Nancy.

"Jordan!" Bess said. "Do you really believe he thinks I'm beautiful?"

"I think Jordan really meant to compliment

you, if that's what you mean," Nancy answered. "I don't know if he meant anything more, though."

"He and Kate seem pretty tight," Bess acknowledged with a sigh. Then she changed the subject.

"Who do you think is responsible for the accidents, Nan?"

"I've already got quite a few suspects on my list," Nancy replied. "People who have real motives for sabotaging this play. Kate, obviously, is one of them. And Hugh, I'm afraid, is also on the list. If he's really upset about Carlos not producing his play, he could be the one causing the trouble."

"Okay—who else?" Bess asked.

"Our friendly publicist, Stella Brentman. She has a lot to lose if the company goes under—but she seems perfectly capable of staging a publicity stunt or two. And, I suppose," Nancy added after a pause, "that Carlos has a lot at stake, too. I'd have to say he's a suspect as well."

"I'm glad I'm coming with you to the hospital," Bess said. "Maybe you shouldn't be alone with Carlos."

"That's what I was thinking, too," Nancy admitted.

Nancy didn't want to admit her other worry to her friend—her concern about Bess's safety. Until Nancy knew who was behind the "accident," Nancy wasn't leaving Bess alone for a minute.

"Thanks, guys, for coming along," Carlos said, after Nancy and Bess had arrived, met the director in the hospital lobby, and then gone upstairs to Zoe's room together.

Carlos knocked on the door of the private room at the end of the corridor.

"Come in!" Zoe's voice was loud. "Carlos!" she gushed, reaching out her uninjured arm to embrace him.

Nancy stood behind Carlos and looked around. An enormous arrangement of pink lilies and white snapdragons overwhelmed the nightstand. On the other side of the bed was an untouched dinner tray.

After Carlos and Zoe greeted each other, Zoe looked up at Nancy and Bess.

"Oh—hello," Zoe said in a chilly tone.

"You look like you're feeling a whole lot better," Bess said enthusiastically. Nancy could see that Zoe had applied makeup—and lots of it.

"I *am* feeling a whole lot better," Zoe said emphatically, gesturing expansively with her arm. As she did so, the bed jacket slipped from her shoulder and revealed a sling that held her injured arm. Zoe winced and quickly pulled the jacket around her.

"But you look like you're in pain," Carlos observed.

"I'll be fine," Zoe snapped. "As soon as I get another pillow to rest my arm. I called the nurse ten minutes ago, and she hasn't bothered to come by."

"I can get you a pillow," Bess volunteered.

"That would be wonderful, dear," Zoe said. She gave Bess a fake smile. "Could you do it right away?"

"Sure," Bess said. She hurried away, shutting the door quietly behind her.

"I'm so sorry about the accident," Nancy said.

"Oh, it's nothing. I'm healing perfectly," Zoe replied. "I'm scheduled to get out of here tomorrow—and you know what that means." She batted her eyes at Carlos, who looked baffled.

"Why don't you tell me," he said, sitting lightly on the edge of the bed.

"I can take back my part—if you'll have me," Zoe said coyly.

Carlos shifted uncomfortably. "You're

really dedicated," he said evenly, "and I'm sure you'll be able to take over soon enough, but I think Bess had better do the first few performances, at least."

Zoe's face fell. "But people are coming to see *me.* The play has a much better chance with me in it than—than with her!" Zoe's voice rose.

"You're absolutely right," Carlos admitted. "But your arm is immobile right now. And that's why I'm asking you to sit things out."

Zoe thought for a moment, then took a new tack. "Listen, Carlos," she said. Nancy detected a frantic note in her voice. "I didn't rehearse around the clock for three weeks just to get passed over for a *nobody.* You *have* to let me open the show—you owe it to me! And besides, this little accident could be just the shot in the arm my career needed."

"Now, Zoe," Carlos said calmly. "I know the show could help your career, but—"

"It's your fault this happened," Zoe cut in. "I ought to sue you for letting it happen!"

"I didn't let anything happen!" Carlos said. Zoe was something else; Nancy could see that Carlos was struggling to keep his patience. The actress certainly sounded desperate—

desperate enough to get herself shot in the arm? Nancy wondered.

"Well, if you're not responsible for the gun slip-up, then who is?" Zoe demanded shrilly.

"I've talked to Hugh about it—if that's what you mean," Carlos said defensively.

"I finally found a fresh pillow," Bess called out as she walked in. "I had to go to the fifth floor to get it."

The actress snatched the pillow from Bess's hand. "Don't expect me to be grateful," she said spitefully. "After all, you've wanted to steal the lead from the very first day of rehearsals."

"What are you talking about?" Bess said, shocked.

"You've been watching me and Jordan like a hawk, waiting for the right opportunity," the actress went on. "I know your type."

"Zoe, that's enough," Carlos cut her off. "Bess was doing no such thing."

Before he could say anything more, the door of the hospital room opened, and an enormous bouquet of flowers was thrust inside. Behind it, Nancy could just make out the form of Stella Brentman.

"Zoe! Sweetheart! You look so bedraggled!" Stella moaned dramatically. Then, all at once, her tone changed. "Will somebody please take these from me?" she demanded, holding out the bouquet.

Carlos took the roses from her, and Stella immediately turned to Zoe, kissing her on both cheeks with a loud smacking noise. "Zoe!" she said breathlessly. "You have no idea how dreadful your fans feel about your loathsome accident!" Zoe listened silently, a frown on her face.

Suddenly, as if she'd run out of sympathetic things to say, Stella wheeled around and flashed Carlos an enormous smile. "Now," she said, "do you want to hear my news?"

Carlos looked around nervously, then smiled. "Of course." He took his publicist by the elbow. "Please, Stella, outside—Zoe needs her rest."

"Oh! I see," Stella said. It was clear to Nancy, too, that Carlos didn't want Zoe to hear what Stella was about to say.

Stella and Carlos backed out into the hallway. Nancy's eyes followed them. So did Bess's. A second later, Nancy's attention was brought back to Zoe.

"Get out of here!" she snapped. "It makes me furious just looking at you!" Zoe leaned back against the pillow and shut her eyes.

Nancy grabbed Bess's arm. "Come on, Bess. Let's go." She could tell that her friend was feeling worse by the minute.

As the two of them went out into the hallway, Nancy gasped at the sight in front of her.

Locked in an embrace in the corridor were Stella and Carlos. The director was smiling widely as the publicist whispered something in his ear.

As Nancy and Bess drew closer to the couple, Nancy could make out some of Stella's words.

"It's going to be the biggest sensation in Chicago theater history," Stella murmured. The director drank in her words. "Ever since the story about the shooting ran on the evening news, the telephone hasn't stopped ringing. We've already sold out the first week, Carlos—we're going to be a smash hit!"

Carlos's smile grew wider. The two of them still hadn't noticed Nancy and Bess. "Are you thinking what I'm thinking?" Carlos asked Stella.

"You mean, that we'll have to extend the run?" Stella responded excitedly. "The thought had crossed my mind. . . ."

Nancy watched the pair, her suspicions mounting. Carlos needed this play to do well, and all Stella Brentman seemed to care about was publicity. Nancy was convinced the publicist would go to almost any length to get media attention. Could the two of them be hatching a plot to make *Mystery Loves Company* a hit?

"Bess and Nancy!" Carlos cried as he spotted them. "Have you heard the good news?"

"Just this second." Nancy forced a smile. "Congratulations."

"I only wish Zoe hadn't had to get hurt for it to happen," Carlos said, sounding a little guilty.

"She looks pretty good," Nancy said. "Luckily the wound isn't very serious."

"Listen, why don't we all go out for a quick dinner to celebrate?" Carlos suggested.

Nancy nodded. It would give her a chance to ask more questions.

"Sure," Bess said.

"Not me." Stella shook her head. "I've got work to do. We want to get you on all the local talk shows next week, darling." She kissed Carlos on both cheeks, waved to the girls, and with a final "*Ciao* for now!" floated off toward the elevators.

Nancy was disappointed Stella wasn't coming, but at least she'd get to question Carlos.

"Shall we?" the director asked, offering each girl an arm. "I don't know about you two, but I'm starving!"

Rick's Café was packed and noisy. Carlos found the manager, who quickly cleared a table for them. Nancy saw the other diners glancing at Carlos and whispering.

"Word certainly has gotten around," Carlos said, smiling nervously.

They were midway through dinner when they heard a murmur go through the restaurant. Nancy looked up to see Jordan making his way among the tables.

Catching sight of him, Bess stood and waved. "Gerald," she called, using his character's name, "over here!"

Jordan waved back. He said something to the manager, then walked over to them. "Hi, everyone," he said. "I heard the good news about the show. Looks like we've got it made. How's Zoe?" he asked a moment later.

"Back to her old self, I'd say," Carlos told him. "She threw quite a tantrum, in fact." He shook his head. "She actually accused Bess of wanting her part all along."

Jordan sighed. "That's crazy," he said. "Bess is far too lovely to compete like that."

Nancy glanced at Bess, who smiled at Jordan. "I tried to tell her I wasn't going for her role," Bess said.

Jordan shook his head. "Zoe's paranoid sometimes."

"Listen, all of you." Carlos changed the subject. "Let's get back to business. We're having a full dress rehearsal this evening at eight—that's an hour from now. I'd like everyone to concentrate on Bess's scenes. We need to let you and Nancy run your lines a couple of times. We may be sold out before we start, but we've got to give our audience its money's worth."

They all agreed. After the meal and a quick dessert, they returned to the theater.

Nancy, Bess, and Jordan were walking toward the dressing rooms when the costumer appeared and handed something to Jordan. "It's your cat-burglar costume, for the final scene," she told him. "I took in the waist like I was supposed to, but I want you to try it on now, in case I still need to work on it during the first act of rehearsal."

Jordan held it up for the girls to see, and Nancy got a close-up view of it for the first time: it was a black spandex outfit, complete with mask. "The audience won't even recognize me in this," Jordan joked.

"Try it on," the costumer urged. Jordan disappeared with the outfit, and Nancy hurried with Bess into the dressing room.

After a few quick run-throughs of Nancy's and Bess's lines, full dress rehearsal was about to begin. Nancy could feel an air of excitement and anticipation surrounding the whole cast and crew. News of the ticket sales had bolstered everyone's spirits; the atmosphere was electric.

When Nancy first stepped onstage, she felt blinded by the intensity of the lights. But as the play progressed, she grew accustomed to the brightness and got through her scenes without incident.

Bess was even more convincing than she had been earlier in the day, although she still forgot her lines when Jordan kissed her. Nancy hoped her friend's performance would be brilliant on opening night. If she wasn't perfect—or close to it—the whole play would drag, and Nancy feared that Carlos would consider replacing Bess.

When the final shooting scene took place, Nancy found herself tensing again, despite the fact that Jordan was still using his finger for a gun. In fact, Nancy noted, there would be a new gun needed for the following night's performance, since the police had taken the original revolver. Nancy made a mental note to check that weapon at intermission every night. Whatever else happened, no one was going to hurt Bess—not while Nancy was around!

After the rehearsal, the cast and crew were visibly exhausted, and Carlos sent them home for a good night's sleep. "We start at noon tomorrow," he informed them. "So rest up and come back ready to go. We're going to work our hearts out tomorrow, and when we're done, we'll give the performance of our lives!"

The cast seemed buoyed by the director's pep talk. Nancy and Bess walked to Nancy's Mustang and began the long drive home.

Bess was excited but nervous, too. "Nan, do you think I'll do all right tomorrow night?" she asked as they sped down the highway leading out of Chicago.

"You'll be incredible, Bess," Nancy assured her. "Chicago's really going to wake up and take notice."

Bess sighed. "Well, even if they can't stand me, and I never get to act again, at least I'll be able to say I kissed Jordan McCabe in front of thousands of witnesses."

"You two really do look good up there together," Nancy told her friend.

"It's too bad about Kate," Bess said, frowning. "She really seems jealous of anyone who gets near Jordan."

"And anyone who gets a part in the play," Nancy added. "So do you think it was Kate who put the real bullets in the gun?" Bess asked.

"I don't know," Nancy said. "As I told you before, she's definitely on my list of suspects. But so are Carlos and Hugh."

"Carlos seemed awfully happy at the hospital earlier when Stella told him about how strong the ticket sales were," Bess acknowledged.

Nancy nodded. "He could have loaded the gun—maybe with Stella's help—to get publicity for the play and the theater. Carlos told us that Stella had a chunk of money invested in the company."

"Carlos is so charming and nice—it's hard to imagine," Bess said. "But Hugh seems nice, too."

"They're all theater people," Nancy reminded her friend. "They're used to acting."

She cast a sidelong glance at Bess. "This may not be what you want to hear, but Jordan could be the one, too. He fired the gun, after all. And he wanted Kate in the part."

"Oh, come on," Bess scoffed. "No way is Jordan McCabe a criminal, Nan—he's way too cute!"

Nancy didn't argue, knowing it would be useless. Bess's crushes had a history of making her blind to people's faults.

Nancy and Bess were silent for the rest of the drive to River Heights, each lost in thought. Finally, Nancy pulled the Mustang in front of Bess's house.

"Want to come in for a minute?" Bess asked.

"No thanks, Bess," Nancy said, yawning. "I've got to get some sleep so I'll be ready for my big performance tomorrow."

Bess smiled. "Okay." She turned around to grab her heavy duffel bag and another bag of makeup.

"I'll help you carry those," Nancy offered. Nancy grabbed one bag and Bess took the other. They headed past the front hedge and onto the porch. Nancy noticed a large manila envelope lying at the foot of the door.

Bess saw it, too. She bent down to pick it up. "It's for me—I wonder what it could be."

Nancy watched as Bess pulled something from the envelope. "It's a photo," Bess said. As she pulled it out completely, Nancy could see that it was the head shot of Bess, the same one that was on display outside the Remington Theater.

Suddenly, Bess gasped and let the photo flutter to the ground. Nancy knelt to pick it up. Her breath caught in her throat. Bess's picture had deep slashes cut into it—and it was smeared with crimson streaks of blood!

Chapter Six

NANCY FOUGHT BACK a brief moment of panic. She glanced around quickly to make sure no one was lurking in the darkness.

When she was satisfied, she examined the photo of Bess more closely under the porch light. Finally, she brought the picture to her face and sniffed. "Peanut butter," she said under her breath.

"Peanut butter?" Bess repeated. "I don't get it, Nan."

"This isn't real blood, Bess; it's stage blood. Specifically, corn syrup, peanut butter, and a little red food coloring."

"Sounds almost good enough to eat." Bess laughed nervously.

Nancy didn't smile. "Whoever did this was sending you a warning, Bess—a warning not to play your part tomorrow night."

"I know," Bess said quietly. She gazed again at her ruined picture. "Somebody really hates me."

"It's a pretty dramatic way of making a point," Nancy admitted. "But it's a lot better than if they'd tried to hurt you physically. Whoever sent this knows how to make stage blood, too. That means they probably have something to do with the theater."

Nancy examined the envelope. It was an ordinary manila envelope with a silver clasp. There was no identification on it or any other clue that might reveal who planted it.

"So what do we do next?" Bess asked anxiously.

Nancy gave her friend what she hoped was a comforting smile. "We do what we were just about to do, before we were so rudely interrupted—we try to get a good night's sleep," she said firmly.

"Sleep? I don't think I'll ever sleep again!"

"You've got a big day tomorrow," Nancy reminded her. "I don't think you should let anyone spoil it for you."

"You're right, Nan," Bess said, giving her a

hug before going inside. "I'll try to concentrate on the play and get some sleep."

As she got back into her car, Nancy couldn't help wondering who among her cast of suspects was brutal enough to spook the new leading lady on the eve of opening night.

Probably the same person who'd been cold-blooded enough to replace blanks with real bullets, she decided.

Nancy stood backstage, in costume, as Bess and Jordan performed their final, fatal scene together. She could see Jordan, in his cat-burglar costume, holding the gun. Suddenly, he raised it and pointed it at Bess.

Tension crackled through the air as Jordan and Bess continued firing their lines back and forth. Then it hit Nancy. Every instinct told her to grab the gun. It was loaded with real bullets again!

Nancy sprang into action. But just as she bolted on stage, strong arms grabbed her from behind. She watched in horror as Jordan cocked the gun, spoke his final line, and—

BANG!

Nancy awoke with a start, springing straight up in bed. "Bess! No!" she shouted, before she realized it had all been a dream.

Nancy took a few deep breaths, trying to calm her thumping heart. She nearly jumped out of her skin when her alarm clock went off a second later.

Finally, Nancy got up and washed her face with cold water. It was time to get going. She and Bess had a long drive ahead of them. It was only a dream, she told herself. But still the play's final scene haunted her.

At nine o'clock Nancy drove to Bess's house to pick up her friend. Bess ran out to the car and plunked herself down on the seat next to Nancy. "I've got to tell you about this weird dream I had, Nan," she said, breathless. "I was totally terrified."

"What was it, Bess?" Nancy asked her friend, startled.

"I was onstage," Bess said, "and it was the first performance, and everyone was so excited . . . and then . . . and then—I couldn't remember my lines!"

Nancy relaxed. So Bess's dream had just been about stage fright.

"Can you believe it, Nan?" Bess went on. "I forgot every one of my lines. What if that really happens?"

"Don't worry, Bess," Nancy said, smiling.

"The only line you've been forgetting is the one after Jordan kisses you."

"Oh, that's one line I won't forget," Bess assured her with a smile. "I wrote it on the cuff of my costume sleeve. I decided I shouldn't take a chance."

Nancy laughed. "I've got to hand it to you, Bess," she said. "You think of everything."

"I learned it from you, Ms. Drew," Bess replied with a smile.

As they pulled into the lot near the theater, Nancy did a double take. There was a large sign in the box office window that was marked Entire Run Sold Out. Several disappointed-looking people were milling about in front of the theater, gazing at the posters for *Mystery Loves Company.* Nancy and Bess hurried over.

"This is so exciting!" Bess gripped Nancy's arm. "I still can't believe this is happening."

Nancy felt Bess's grip tighten on her arm. "Now we know where that photo of me came from," Bess said.

Nancy followed her friend's gaze to the display case. Bess's head shot was missing. It had been there yesterday, Nancy remembered clearly. She touched the glass and noted that the case was unlocked. Any passerby could have easily removed the photo, she reasoned. But that didn't explain who had gone to Bess's home and delivered the ominous message.

"Good thing I brought another one," Bess said, smiling slyly. She pulled it out of her bag and clipped it to the board. "There."

As they opened the doors, Nancy heard shouting coming from inside the theater. Kate Grenoble was standing on the stage with Carlos, shouting at him while the cast and crew looked on.

"What do you mean, no?" she cried. "I'm offering you the services of a well-known, proven actress in place of an inexperienced amateur!"

"Please try to understand, Kate," Carlos replied levelly. "Bess is the understudy for Zoe. She's been living with the part—she's rehearsed it, prepared for it."

"So have I!" Kate shot back. "Jordan and I have worked on every single scene together!" Suddenly, realizing what she had said, she added, "I mean, just in case. Not that we knew anything would happen to Zoe."

Or did you? Nancy wondered.

"Look, I already told you, there's nothing I can do." Carlos held firm. "I'm using Bess because she knows the lines—and she can act." He turned around and added under his breath, "Which is more than I can say for some people."

"What! I heard that." Kate's face went beet red, and her hands were balled up into tight fists. "That is a total insult, Carlos! I . . . I—never mind!" She stormed offstage and up the aisle, heading right for Nancy and Bess, with Jordan behind her.

"If it isn't the leading lady!" Kate sneered as she passed Bess. "Good luck tonight," she added sarcastically. "I hope you—"

"That's enough, Kate!" Jordan warned her. "Bess, I'm sorry," he called, as he followed Kate out the door to the lobby.

Bess stood quietly until Carlos called out, "Let's go, everybody. We need to get started, Jordan or no Jordan."

The rehearsal began. Nancy went through her scene, with Carlos himself stepping in for Jordan. Jordan returned for the next scene, not bothering to explain his absence. Instead, he hopped right into his first scene with Bess.

After Nancy had finished her lines in the first act, she decided to investigate the backstage areas of the theater. She wasn't due back onstage until the final scene of the second act—she could take her time exploring all the dark nooks and crannies she'd seen only briefly before.

I've spent so much time concentrating on the suspects and my acting, Nancy realized, *I haven't given the theater building itself a good going over.* Maybe she could learn something more about how the fire started.

Nancy walked quietly to the rear of the house and opened the trapdoor leading to the circuit box. Soundlessly, she descended to the level below the theater, where she followed a hallway that led beneath the stage. A maze of passages revealed storage space for old props and set pieces. Above her, Nancy saw a trap-door in what she knew was the floor of the stage. It was boarded shut now, but it must have been used in previous productions.

Nancy froze. A shuffling noise came from nearby. She crouched down and took cover, behind some scenery. The shuffling noise came again. It seemed to be coming from another staircase on the other side of the stage. Nancy crept closer.

When she reached the staircase, she slowly began to climb the steps. She drew back as she noticed a shadow playing against the wall. The shadow wavered in the half-light, and then a figure came into view.

"Hugh!" Nancy gasped. "What are you doing here?"

"I . . . uh. I, well—" He looked around, as if searching for a way out of his embarrassment. "I—I came to return Carlos's keys," he stammered, "and then came down here to pick up some stuff I left in the prop area." He held up a shirt.

"So why were you hiding from me, if you were just here to pick up some clothing?" Nancy asked him.

In the darkness she could see him biting his lip. "I don't want Carlos to find me here. He'd blow another gasket, you know?" He smiled weakly.

Nancy had to agree that was true—Carlos would certainly be furious at the sight of Hugh. But Nancy still didn't quite believe the stage manager. His being here, hiding this way, seemed suspicious to her.

"Well, I've got to get up there," Nancy told him, as she turned to retrace her steps. "My final scene is coming up. Excuse me."

Nancy hurried down the passageway and back upstairs.

In the theater, everyone's attention was riveted on the action, as Bess and Jordan played out their first big confrontation.

Nancy saw that Bess had relaxed since the drama began: Her movements looked even more natural, and her voice was clear and strong. She stepped backward gracefully to take a book out of the bookcase behind her.

Nancy blinked. For a moment, she thought she'd seen the bookcase shift a fraction of an inch. Had she imagined it? She quickly ran her gaze around the perimeter of the bookcase. She knew the stagehands had bolted the case to the wall behind it.

Then it happened again. The bookcase shifted. But before Nancy could move or call out a warning, the top of the bookcase tore away from its bolts. One moment more and it would topple—right onto the leading lady!

Chapter Seven

NANCY SPRANG INTO ACTION. She took a running leap at Bess, tackling her. Both of them fell to the floor in a heap, just as the bookcase came crashing down beside them, missing them by inches!

Jordan came running. "Are you two all right?" His eyes were wide with fright.

Stagehands and cast members gathered around as Bess and Nancy sat up.

"Thanks, Nan. That was a close call," Bess said in a shaky voice.

"What in the world is happening around this place?" Carlos's voice boomed. The crowd parted to let him through. "Is everyone okay?" he asked, crouching down in front of them.

"We're fine," Nancy told him. "But somebody should check on how that bookcase was attached to the wall."

"I already have," said Hugh, coming up behind them.

"You!" Carlos jumped to his feet and grabbed Hugh by the collar of his shirt. "What are you still doing here?"

"I had to clean up some stuff downstairs. When I heard the commotion, I ran up here. You may have fired me, but I still care about this production."

"I'll bet this was your handiwork, Hugh," the director accused him. "The police are investigating everything—you won't get away with this."

"I'm going to ignore that remark," Hugh said. He shook off Carlos's grasp. Nancy couldn't help noticing the change in him. Before being fired, he had never stood up to Carlos like that.

"Here's what happened, in case you're interested," Hugh continued. "The bolts on top—where the bookcase was attached to the flat—were apparently loose. That's how it pulled away from the brick wall. The brick is crumbling, too. So the whole flat had no support at all."

"Where's Tim Talcott?" Carlos bellowed.

"Somebody call me?" Tim's voice sounded from the back of the house. He came up onto the stage, and Carlos explained what had just happened.

"Hugh here is implying that the accident happened because your building's falling apart," he finished.

"Is that right?" Tim said. He stared at Hugh, surprised to see him. "Let's have a look, then, shall we?"

As Hugh led the men behind the set, Nancy followed. Hugh pointed to the spot high on the brick wall where the bolts and cable had torn loose. Nancy heard a crunching noise as she walked over the crumbled brick that littered the floor.

"It seems that Hugh has a point, Tim," Jordan said, poking the debris with his shoe.

"Look," Tim said, turning to Carlos. "I do my best to keep this place in good repair. It's an old building, and there's only me to look after the place. Carlos, if you want to get out of your lease and find another place for your theater company, I would certainly understand. I'm sure I'd have trouble getting another tenant like you—but I'd try if it would help the Remington. . . ."

Carlos smiled and patted Tim on the back. "I can't afford to do anything right now, Tim, but maybe in the future," he said. "We've got a long lease here, and you've given us very favorable terms. Besides, the neighborhood's picking up, getting very popular. I have a hunch this is going to be the perfect place to be long-term. I guess we'll have to live with the occasional problem. But please, Tim—let's take care of the real hazards. Somebody's going to get hurt here if you don't watch out."

Tim kept his good humor. "Sorry, all of you," he said. "I'll do my best to see that it doesn't happen again."

Carlos turned his attention to the cast and crew. "Come on, people," he said. "Let's get that set repaired and get back to work. We've got a show to do!"

Nancy helped Bess offstage and down the hall to their dressing room. Bess was still shaken but otherwise okay. "Nan," she said, "last night's package seems harmless compared to this. You don't think Hugh was responsible for that bookcase falling, do you?"

"I don't know, Bess," Nancy replied. "Carlos seemed to accept the explanation that the building's old—maybe that's true."

"At least we know it couldn't have been Zoe," Bess said with a chuckle. "She's still in the hospital."

Nancy decided she'd check with the hospital, just to make sure that was true. But as it turned out, she didn't need to call. No sooner had the cast resumed the rehearsal than Zoe appeared.

Nancy watched in awe as the former star of the show barged through the theater doors and stormed down the aisle.

Bess and Jordan, who were trying to get through their final scene, stopped and turned to look.

"Oh, do go on—don't mind me," Zoe directed, sitting down in a front-row seat. Her arm was still in its sling, Nancy noticed, but here she was in the theater. Could she possibly have gotten someone to loosen the bookcase and pull the screws from the wall? Someone like Hugh?

Carlos came out from backstage. "What is it now?" he demanded. Then he saw Zoe sitting there in the front row. "Zoe—hello! Welcome back. Feeling better?"

"Much better," Zoe said, seething. She stood up and started waving her good arm around. "In fact, I'm ready to take my part back right now!"

"Zoe," Carlos said, "take it easy, please." He jumped down off the stage and took her by the shoulders. "We've been through this already. I can't have you onstage in a sling—it changes the whole play. You'll just have to wait a few weeks—"

"Until when the reviews are out?" Zoe interrupted, pulling away from him. "Until the run is almost over? Forget it! I'm an actress, Carlos—not an understudy!"

"Sorry, Zoe, there's nothing I can do. And that's final." Carlos turned away from her and back toward the stage. "Take it from where we left off, guys," he said to Jordan and Bess.

Nancy watched from her perch backstage left. Zoe followed Carlos for a few steps, and Nancy thought she could almost see the steam coming out of the actress's ears.

Then, suddenly, a flash went off, and Nancy's gaze shifted to the rear of the house, where Stella stood in the middle of a group of photographers. Nancy noticed one photographer shooting Bess.

What a coincidence, Nancy thought. Stella arrives right after Zoe—and right in the middle of the fight between Zoe and Carlos!

Nancy could see it all now: more headlines in the afternoon papers, more rumors and gossip about the hottest new show in town. Stella was good at what she did, Nancy had to admit.

The big question was, just how far would the publicist go to get attention?

With all the commotion, it was a wonder that Bess and Jordan were able to play their final scene at all. Still, they got through it.

At the point where Bess staggered and fell, Nancy's heart skipped a beat; her friend had done a truly realistic job of it.

Go for it, Bess! she thought as she watched. Her friend was going to be a smash in the role—provided she got the chance to perform it.

Jordan motioned tossing away the gun and went to pour himself a brandy. It was Nancy's cue. She stepped onstage and said, "I was just about to put away the linens, and I heard a—" Nancy looked down and saw Bess lying there. She paused a moment to register what had happened. Then she and Jordan both raced for the imaginary gun. Nancy got there first and pointed her finger at Jordan. "Sorry, Mr. Harbinger," she said, "but it's curtains for you."

The lights dimmed and went black. There was applause from backstage and the house. The run-through was over.

"House lights up!" Carlos shouted. The lights came back on, and everyone gathered together on the stage.

"Okay, people," Carlos told them, "we're looking good. It's nearly three o'clock. I want you to take some time now—your call is at six-thirty. If you can, try to relax so you have something left for tonight."

Bess pulled Nancy offstage and whispered, "How did I do? Did I look okay?"

"You're going to be fabulous, Bess," Nancy assured her.

"Just keep away from falling bookcases, okay?"

Bess nodded, then said, "How about Zoe Adams? She's unbelievable. And Kate, too. It's so crazy that these actresses are jealous of me! *Me,* Bess Marvin, from River Heights. It's unreal."

"It sure is," Nancy agreed. But in her heart of hearts, she knew it was very, very real. And so was the danger. Hugh and Carlos seemed to believe that the accident was caused just by the old building. But Nancy had a hunch that someone had wanted that bookcase to fall on Bess. Luckily, they'd failed this time. But surely they would try again, and soon.

"Why don't I meet you at Rick's for lunch?" Nancy said. "I need to call home. I forgot to tell Hannah what time we'd be back tonight."

Bess agreed and took off for Rick's. Nancy headed out to the lobby telephones. The booths were the old-fashioned kind, with doors for privacy. Working in an old building wasn't all bad, Nancy thought.

Nancy entered a booth, pulled the door closed, dialed her home number, and spoke briefly with the Drews' housekeeper, Hannah Gruen.

As she was about to open the door of the booth, she realized that someone was talking in the booth next to hers. Her detective's instincts told her to hold perfectly still and listen.

The voice she heard through the wall of the booth was Jordan McCabe's. It was muffled, but Nancy could make out what he was saying, all right.

"I don't want her killed." The words sent a

chill up Nancy's spine. She crouched down to avoid being seen as she waited to hear more.

"Please," Jordan was begging. "I don't want her killed. Isn't there some other way?" There was a long pause while he listened to the voice on the other end of the phone.

Nancy's heart raced. Who was Jordan talking about?

"I understand. Okay, if that's the way it has to be, I guess I have to go along."

Panic was rising in Nancy's throat. Jordan was planning something—but what and with whom?

"Fine," Jordan said. "But please—try not to hurt her too much. She's suffered enough already."

He hung up, opened the door of the phone booth, and walked away. Nancy knew she was out of sight, but her heart was pounding like a jackhammer.

It sounded as though Jordan was in on a plan to kill someone. Was that someone Bess?

Chapter Eight

NANCY FLUNG OPEN the door of the booth and raced up the stairs. She had to find Jordan and learn what was going on. She peeked through the theater doors, but the house was as empty as the lobby. Nancy turned and went outside.

Her gaze took in the sidewalk in both directions. Jordan was obviously moving quickly; he was nowhere in sight. Nancy wondered for a second where he had gone. Then she remembered that Bess was at Rick's, waiting for her. She had to get there soon, or Bess would be worried.

Rick waved to Nancy when she entered the café. By now, the owner knew her. She waved back, then located Bess in the rear of the restaurant. Jordan was standing over her, smiling.

Nancy's insides lurched. She couldn't let Jordan harm her friend.

The place was bustling as usual, and Nancy had to work her way through the crowd milling around the coffee bar.

"Hi, Bess. Jordan," she said cordially, looking from leading man to leading lady and back again.

"You all right, Nan?" Bess said, studying Nancy's face. "You look funny."

"Everything's fine," Nancy tried to reassure her.

Jordan smiled at Bess, and took her hand in his. "I just came in myself," he said, "and Bess was kind enough to invite me to join you two for a bite. Otherwise, I'd have to wait my turn like everyone else."

"Fat chance," Bess said, laughing. "You know you would have gotten a table no matter what. You're a VIP, Jordan."

"You will be, too, Bess, after tonight," he told her.

"Excuse me, Jordan," Nancy broke in before Jordan could sit down. "Could you possibly give me a hand? I'm having a problem with my car—one of my tires looks flat and I'd rather deal with it now instead of later, after dark."

Bess gave Nancy a surprised look.

"Sure, Nancy." Jordan shrugged. "Will you excuse us for a minute, Bess? Come on, Nancy, we can go out through the back door."

"I'll meet you back here in a few minutes," Bess told them. "I'm headed for the restroom anyway." She headed for the ladies' room, casting a curious backward glance at Nancy. She didn't ask what was going on, but she clearly knew something was up.

"Can I be straight with you?" Nancy asked Jordan once they were outside.

"Of course," Jordan said, looking confused.

"I overheard you on the phone a few minutes ago." When Jordan gave her a blank look, Nancy added, "Something about how 'if she has to be killed, I'll go along with it. . . .' Does that sound familiar?"

Jordan's eyes widened. "Oh, that!" he said. "Who did you think I was out to get?"

"A friend of mine," Nancy said flatly.

Suddenly, Jordan laughed out loud. "Nancy, you couldn't have thought I was plotting to kill Bess!"

"The thought did cross my mind," Nancy

admitted, folding her arms to await his explanation.

"I was talking with my agent—who also happens to be Kate's agent." The smile left Jordan's face suddenly. "He was telling me they're killing off Kate's character on the soap. Kate doesn't know yet, and when she does, she's going to be devastated."

"Oh." Nancy's whole body relaxed. For a moment, she nearly laughed at the absurdity of her misunderstanding. Then she got serious again. His explanation sounded plausible, but how did she know he was telling the truth? Jordan McCabe is an actor, she reminded herself. A very talented one.

"So I guess it would be a lifesaver for Kate if she got the part opposite you in the play," Nancy said, trying to draw him out.

"Of course," Jordan admitted. "I tried to talk Carlos into using Kate when we were just starting out, but he was set on Zoe. Then I tried again to convince him after Zoe got shot, but he had already decided on Bess." Jordan shook his head, then continued smoothly. "Carlos is the director. The casting is up to him. I put in my bid for Kate, then I backed off."

"I understand," Nancy said patiently. "And

if something should suddenly happen to Bess . . . like a bookcase falling on her . . ."

"Now wait a minute, Nancy," Jordan jumped in, picking right up on her meaning. "I would never do anything to hurt Bess. She's a great girl, and she's doing a fantastic job, considering everything that's happened—and that she's never been in such a big production. But the truth is, I do wish it were Kate I was kissing up there."

"You really care for her, then," Nancy said, seeing the concern in his eyes and hearing it in his voice.

"I'm pretty crazy about her," Jordan admitted, nodding.

Nancy found herself feeling moved by his feelings for Kate. But she also knew from her years of detective work to trust her instincts. And at this point her instincts were reminding her that Jordan's love for Kate only strengthened his motivation to sabotage the production in order to get Kate a role. It was possible that Jordan was just putting on another performance for Nancy's benefit. Nancy felt shaken by the thought.

A minute later Nancy and Jordan returned to Rick's. Bess had ordered sandwiches and iced tea for the three of them. Nancy said little, letting Bess take the lead in the conversation. She considered warning Bess about Jordan, but it might be better to wait until later. With opening night, Bess already had enough to worry about.

Nancy vowed to stay quiet for now and stay alert. Whoever was striking out at the leading ladies would probably make another move soon.

Nancy and Bess spent the rest of the afternoon strolling around the neighborhood. To Nancy's relief, Bess seemed to have forgotten Nancy's asking Jordan about the car—she didn't want to go into it with Bess and worry her needlessly on opening night.

Finally they returned to the theater to prepare for the performance. When the actors had assembled, Carlos told them they would run through the final scene first. The assistant stage manager had brought in a new prop gun, and the cast rehearsed the shooting scene over and over. Nancy's ears were ringing from all the shots, and she was sure everyone else's were, too.

After each go-through, Nancy made a point of inspecting the gun. At each scene break, she slid backstage inconspicuously, never letting the weapon leave her sight. While Jordan held it, her eyes followed him back and forth across the stage.

When their last pre-show break arrived, Nancy suggested to Bess that they take a quick stroll around the block. Nancy needed to walk off her nervousness. They slipped out the back door and down the block.

"How are you feeling?" Nancy asked.

"Ready," Bess said, and flashed Nancy an eager grin. "Ready as I'll ever be, anyway." Bess's expression suddenly changed. "But I've got to tell you, Nan, I'm scared. So much has happened. I really admire the way you've been so cool about it all."

Nancy smiled her thanks.

Bess chattered on. "I've got to be as calm as you are—I just can't mess up tonight! This could be the beginning of a whole career for me, you know? Not that I even know if I want it. But it would be so great if everybody liked me, wouldn't it?"

"They're going to," Nancy reassured her friend. "And try not to worry about anything but your acting, Bess—I'm looking out for you."

"I know," Bess said, leaning over and giving Nancy a quick hug. "You always do. You're the best, Drew."

"So are you," Nancy said, lost in thought. She brightened for a moment. "Are your parents coming into town to see you?" she asked.

"Uh-huh," Bess said. "But I told them to wait till next week to come see me—I got them tickets for next Friday just in case I'm not my best tonight. How about you—is your dad coming?"

"I asked him not to," Nancy admitted. "Just the thought of it makes me more nervous."

By the time Nancy and Bess got back to the theater, the entire block had come to life.

"Boy, Carlos is right," said Bess. "This part of town *is* getting popular."

Nancy agreed.

People milled about in front of the galleries and cafés. There was a long line at the doors of the theater itself.

The lights were on in the box office as the harried theater manager tried to explain to people that there were no seats at any price for tonight's show. The marquee announced Jordan McCabe in *Mystery Loves Company.*

"Your name will be up there one of these days, too," Nancy said, her arm around Bess.

"Maybe . . ." Bess said with a smile. "Right now I just hope I live through this night. My stomach feels like there's someone tap dancing inside."

Ahead of them, Nancy spotted Tim Talcott. He was dressed in a navy suit and silk tie.

"You look elegant," Nancy said.

Startled, Tim turned toward the girls.

"Jumpy?" Bess asked.

Tim chuckled and smoothed his hair. "You know how opening night is—nerve-racking," he said.

"You can say that again," Nancy said.

They all entered through the stage door. Nancy and Bess said goodbye to Tim, then headed to the ladies' dressing room. To Bess's delight, there were five bouquets of flowers on her makeup table.

Bess read aloud the cards from Carlos, Jordan, George, and her parents, wishing her well. "Look, Nan—this one's from Hugh," Bess said, admiring the pink and white tulips. "I wish Carlos hadn't fired him and he could be here tonight."

"Me, too," Nancy agreed, looking at the card and flowers at her own spot. "'Best wishes to my favorite acting coach turned actress. You're gonna knock them dead tonight! Love, Carlos,'" Nancy read out loud, and smiled. Guilty or not guilty, Carlos was certainly considerate.

She put the flowers aside and began to lay out her makeup. Just then, there was a knock on the door, and Jordan came in, a worried expression on his face. "I can't find my cat-burglar costume!" he said. "Have either of you seen it?"

Nancy and Bess looked at each other. "Not since you wore it this afternoon," Nancy said. "Are you sure it's missing?"

"The assistant stage manager and I have been looking everywhere for it," Jordan said. He collapsed into a canvas director's chair. "Great. Just great! Now what am I going to do?"

"Hey, don't worry, Jordan," Bess said, snapping her fingers. "I've got a great idea." She sprang to her feet. As Nancy and Jordan watched in astonishment, Bess proceeded to pull out some black clothing and material from under the makeup table. "I noticed this dark fabric and these extra clothes under here the other day—black pants and some dark T-shirts. Jordan, I'm going to throw together a brand-new costume in record time."

"You can really do that?" Jordan asked,

astonished. "Wow! You're multitalented, Bess."

Bess blushed and, without answering, began laying out the fabric on the floor. Jordan knelt down next to her. Soon both of them were completely absorbed in their task.

Nancy caught a quick movement out of the corner of her eye and turned around. There was Kate Grenoble, standing in the open doorway! She was glowering down at Jordan and Bess, clenching and unclenching her fists.

When Kate saw Nancy looking at her, she reddened. Without a word, she turned and stalked off down the hallway. Neither Bess nor Jordan had even noticed her.

Nancy decided to make good use of time. While Jordan and Bess busied themselves with his new costume, she would make one last thorough check of the theater's lower level. Nancy wanted to ensure there were no nasty surprises in the making.

Wearing her maid costume and makeup, Nancy descended the stairs. She was careful not to brush up against any surfaces; the soot in the theater's cellar was bound to show on the white apron she wore.

Nancy reached the bottom of the steps and walked briskly through the passageways she remembered. Soon she found herself staring at a door she hadn't noticed before. It was partially hidden by a canvas flat that lay against it. Nancy moved the flat aside and tried the door. It was unlocked.

The door led her down another corridor. Nancy moved through the dimly lit hallway. She tried to determine where she was and estimated that she was somewhere under the backstage dressing rooms.

Turning a corner, Nancy caught sight of something strange. She stopped to stare at it.

Several boxes had been piled up to create a protective wall. Behind the shelter of the wall was a rolled-up sleeping bag. Next to it she saw a comb, a hair brush, a bar of soap, a washcloth—and some fast-food wrappers.

Nancy blinked in utter surprise. Who did these things belong to? She wondered. Was someone actually living in the theater?

Chapter Nine

NANCY HAD NO TIME to examine her discovery. At that moment she heard the assistant stage manager's voice over the loudspeaker announcing, "Ten-minute call, everybody. Ten minutes, please."

Nancy let out a frustrated sigh. For now her sleuthing would have to wait. She'd have to return later, after her first scene was over.

Nancy hurried up the stairs. At the top, she closed the heavy metal door behind her, making sure to cover it with the flat before returning to her dressing room.

Bess and Jordan were already gone. Nancy assumed they were in position onstage. Although the stage manager hadn't called "places" yet, the actors were likely to jump the gun; it was opening night, and everyone was excited.

Nancy quickly checked herself in the mirror, then headed for the stage. She got to her spot just as "places" was called.

Nancy was surprised at how nervous she felt. *You've been in some really dangerous situations, Drew,* she chided herself. *This is only a play.* But somehow the prospect of being onstage and acting in front of hundreds of paying customers seemed just as frightening as investigating a crime. She couldn't control the butterflies in her stomach.

"Get a grip, Nan." Bess was whispering in her ear. "You look like you've just seen a ghost."

Nancy smiled. "I feel that way—I'm so nervous. How about you?"

"I'm fine," Bess told her. "Ready to get started."

"Good luck," Nancy said.

"Uh-uh." Bess wagged a finger. "Not 'good luck.' 'Break a leg.' That's what we say in the theater, remember?"

They gave each other the thumbs-up sign as the lights in the audience dimmed and the stage lit up. The crowd applauded when they saw Jordan.

It was time. Nancy knocked on the upstage right door and entered, stepping onto the stage with her feather duster in hand. "Pardon me, Mr. Harbinger," she said. "I know how much you dislike interruptions, especially at a time like this. . . ."

"What do you mean—'at a time like this,' Hayley?" Jordan looked up at her, puzzled.

"Oh my, I suppose no one has told you yet," Nancy replied. "Catherine Daniels was found murdered half an hour ago. They found her in the billiard room with a carving knife stuck between her second and third ribs. Made a staggering mess on her white carpet."

There was a ripple of laughter from the audience. Nancy had wondered if her comic line would get a response. Now she knew; she relaxed a bit.

"Oh, dear," Jordan said, getting up from the roll-top desk. He turned to the audience. "How very inconvenient. I certainly don't have time to solve this crime." The audience tittered.

"Well, sir, let me offer my services as an amateur detective! I propose to help you," Nancy said with a smile.

"Why, Hayley," he enthused, "I would be delighted for your assistance. After all," he added, "mystery loves company!"

The audience chuckled as Jordan echoed the title line of the show. For a brief second Nancy's thoughts flashed to the *real* mystery at the Remington Theater. Once again, it struck her that the play was imitating real life. Or was real life imitating the play?

Nancy snapped back to attention. It was Bess's turn to enter. There was a knock at the door, and Jordan opened it. Bess looks beautiful, Nancy couldn't help thinking. The audience actually applauded Bess's entrance.

Nancy understood the crowd's reaction. Everyone out there had read about the shooting of Zoe Adams. They knew all about the young understudy who had assumed the part at the last minute. The audience was rooting for Bess and seemed behind her all the way.

Maybe Stella wasn't all bad, Nancy thought. She certainly had made the most of the strange things happening behind the scenes.

"Xena!" Jordan gasped, as soon as the applause faded. "What are you doing in town?"

"I was passing through on my way to Eden Prairie," Bess said. "Aren't you glad to see me?"

"Of course," Jordan countered, turning so the audience could see his whole face. "What man isn't glad to see his ex-wife?"

At this, the audience exploded with laughter. Nancy felt a thrill go through her. They were loving the performance—and the dramatic, suspenseful parts hadn't even come up yet! Nancy knew it was a good sign. The ending was going to take the crowd completely by surprise. It was Nancy's cue to exit, stage right.

"Excuse me, Mr. Harbinger," Nancy cut in, "I'll be moving along to the study now. Thanks for your time today."

"Don't mention it," Jordan said.

Nancy exited and ran quickly back to her dressing room. She changed into her costume for the final scene of the play. Then she checked the clock on the wall. She had the rest of the first act, all of intermission, and most of the second act. It would be plenty of time to investigate the makeshift living quarters downstairs.

Taking care that nobody noticed her, Nancy made her way down the stairs and along the corridor to the hidden door. But the door was no longer hidden—someone had removed the flat.

Had one of the stagehands needed the flat for some reason? Nancy wondered. Or had the owner of the sleeping bag returned?

Nancy brought out her small flashlight. She walked down the dimly lit corridor to the wall of boxes. Peering around them, she saw, to her relief, that the little hideaway had not been disturbed in her absence.

She quickly checked the items lying next to the sleeping bag. The toothbrush and soap could belong to anyone, she mused, a man or a woman. And they might not even belong to the person who was creating so much trouble at the theater. Still, Nancy thought, if she could solve this piece of the puzzle, she might have a valuable clue.

Nancy picked up the comb and shone her flashlight on it. There were no hairs caught in it, no clues to be found there. Nancy replaced it.

Suddenly, there was a noise in the darkness behind her. Nancy's breath caught in her throat. "Who's there?" she said, whirling around.

But as she turned to face the intruder, a hand clamped down over her mouth. Nancy's scream was silenced as someone tried to drag her away!

Chapter Ten

FOR A MOMENT Nancy couldn't breathe. The muscular arms gripped her tightly. Then a voice in her ear whispered, "Don't be afraid, Nancy, it's only me."

Nancy pried the hand off her mouth and took in a long gulp of air. Spinning around, she aimed her flashlight on her captor's face. It was Hugh!

He raised an arm, and Nancy drew back, positioning herself for self-defense.

"Hey!" Hugh said, shielding his eyes from the light. "I can't see anything!"

Nancy kept the light on his face. "Why did you grab me like that?" she demanded. "You scared me half to death! And what are you doing down here, anyway? You're not supposed to be on the premises anymore."

"Look," Hugh began. "I know. I'm really sorry. I only grabbed you so you wouldn't scream when you saw me. I didn't want the performance to be disturbed. The audience is right over our heads, you know."

"I realize that," Nancy shot back.

"Sorry." Hugh slumped down along the wall until he was sitting on the hallway floor. Nancy lowered herself down across from him.

"This is your stuff I found, isn't it?" she asked him.

Hugh nodded. "I've been . . . well, living here, actually."

"What do you mean, you've been living here? Since when?" Nancy asked.

"For a while," Hugh confessed. "I needed a place to stay." He lowered his eyes. "It was only going to be temporary—for a couple of weeks, until I could find another place."

"Where were you living before you came here?" Nancy asked.

"In a studio apartment," Hugh said. "I was living on my own for a couple of years, but the rent kept going up—and the money I was making here wasn't enough."

"Why didn't you get another job?" Nancy asked.

"I thought working in the theater was a good idea—I'm a playwright," Hugh explained. Nancy said nothing, waiting for him to continue. "Besides, I figured it was only a matter of time before I was out of here. There's a really great writing program at the university here in Chicago. So I applied and actually got accepted. The only problem was, it was going to cost a lot of money."

He sighed. "I thought about moving back in with my parents to save money," he went on.

"Sounds reasonable," Nancy interjected.

"But they live too far away. The commute was impossible. When I first got this job, I thought it would be a real lifesaver," he said. "But that was before Carlos started coming down hard on me, blaming me for everything that went wrong with his precious production."

Hugh's expression turned bitter. "I don't know why he hates me so much. I never did anything to him. I always did my job. I can't help it if this building's falling apart and if someone's deliberately trying to cause trouble. But it was almost like they were doing it just so *I'd* get blamed for it!"

Nancy frowned. She could see how that might be true. But framing Hugh wasn't an end in itself—there had to be another reason for all the trouble. It seemed to her that the stage manager was a convenient person to pin things on—if his story was for real.

"You know that living here is illegal," Nancy said quietly. "Do the police know?"

Hugh shook his head. "I figured I was in enough trouble over the revolver incident. I gave them my parents' address." He added, "If it makes any difference, I only planned to stay here for the run of the show. By then I'd have earned enough money to pay for some expenses—and find a permanent apartment. But I didn't count on getting fired."

He lowered his head again, looking completely dejected. Nancy had a feeling he was telling the truth.

"Maybe you can get some scholarship money," Nancy told him, "and a real apartment. But first we've got to find out what's going on here."

"Believe me, I've tried. I've asked around and turned it over in my mind. But I can't figure out the plot—or the motive—for this one," Hugh said, sounding genuinely perplexed.

"You've been down here the whole time," Nancy said. "Is there anything you've noticed? Anyone hanging around where they weren't supposed to be? Any strange noises?"

Hugh thought for a moment, then shrugged. "Sorry," he told Nancy. "It's just been me down here and the usual people working on the show or the building. But if I think of anything unusual, I'll let you know."

"Good," Nancy said. "Well, I'd better get going. I've got an entrance in a few minutes."

"How's it going up there?" Hugh asked.

"I think we're a hit," Nancy told him.

"And Bess?" Hugh asked eagerly.

"She's a smash." Nancy couldn't help grinning. There was one thing the two of them certainly had in common—they were both big fans of Bess Marvin. "But I'm worried about her, Hugh. You saw what happened with that bookcase. She's a prime target for this troublemaker, whoever that is."

"I know," Hugh said. "That's another reason I've been hanging around this place."

Nancy nodded and got up. "I've gotta go," she said. "We'll talk more later." Nancy ran back down the corridor and through the hidden door.

It was later than she'd thought. To her dismay, she realized that Bess and Jordan were already onstage for the shooting scene. Nancy swallowed, trying not to panic. This time Nancy hadn't had time to check the bullets in the gun!

Jordan already had the revolver in his belt. There was no way Nancy could fake her way onstage to examine the weapon.

There's nothing you can do about it now, she told herself grimly. *That gun is going to be fired. You just have to hope for the best.*

Jordan wore the makeshift cat-burglar costume Bess had rigged up with him just before the show. *It's doing the trick,* Nancy thought, although the mask didn't hide Jordan's face as well as the mask on the original costume.

"I do love you, darling," Jordan was saying, down on his knees. Bess stood in front of him, looking as if she'd been acting this part her whole life.

"Ha!" Bess scoffed.

"I'll prove it to you!" Jordan swept Bess up

in his arms and kissed her passionately. Bess leaned back, surrendering to his embrace.

"How was that?" Jordan asked, as he released her. Bess breathed hard—once, twice—and Nancy feared Bess would forget her line.

But Bess was only milking the moment. "Acceptable, I'd say," she finally declared. The audience laughed and erupted into spontaneous applause.

"I'll do better!" Jordan said, and kissed her again.

There was an audible murmur from the audience. The good-looking TV star had a lot of female fans. And at this moment Bess was the envy of every one of them. Nancy wondered if Kate was in the audience, watching.

"Have you been taking lessons?" Bess asked, incredulous.

"I'm a natural. Now, please," Jordan begged, "let's keep all this talk of blackmail and murder to ourselves."

Nancy watched nervously as the scene continued. Right on cue, Jordan reached for the gun. Nancy tried not to think about the terrifying dream she'd had the night before. "I'll prove it to you," he said. Slowly, he reached for the trigger.

Nancy braced herself for the noise that would come onstage. Instead, a series of ear-splitting bangs exploded somewhere else in the theater—at the rear, behind the audience.

There was a loaded gun in the house—and someone had just opened fire!

Chapter Eleven

NANCY RACED ONSTAGE toward Bess. She knocked her to the floor as the audience broke into panicked screams.

"Everybody get down!" Carlos's voice boomed out through the pandemonium.

"I'm okay," Bess murmured. "I didn't get shot."

"Thank goodness." Nancy breathed out a sigh of relief. She glanced around and saw that nobody else on the stage had been hurt.

It had sounded as if the gunfire came from the main entrance to the theater. Nancy jumped off the stage into the aisle and ran toward the lobby. The area was still filled with acrid-smelling smoke, and members of the audience crouched beside their seats, terrified the shooting would start up again.

Nancy flung open the lobby doors, ready to take cover if she had to. But the lobby was deserted. She ran out into the street; the crowd on the sidewalk was thick. Whoever had fired the gun had either blended into the crowd or gotten away.

Nancy went back through the lobby and into the auditorium again. She scanned the last row of seats, and her eyes landed on the source of the gunfire.

"Firecrackers!" she exclaimed as a crowd started to gather around her.

"Someone has a really warped sense of humor," a man commented. Angry onlookers agreed with him.

"Ladies and gentlemen, please!" Carlos pleaded, his voice ringing out above all the others. "Let's not let a random incident ruin our evening in the theater. The play is at its climactic moment. If you'll all just return to your seats, we can finish the performance and demonstrate that we can't be intimidated by saboteurs."

The audience gave him a hearty round of applause, and soon they were settled again in their seats. Carlos instructed Nancy to start the scene with her entrance.

The scene played itself out in less than a minute. Nancy spotted the gun, beat Jordan to it, held it on him as he backed away, his hands high. In a dramatic tone, she delivered her final line: "Sorry, Mr. Harbinger, but it's curtains for you!"

The lights went down, and the audience burst into one thunderous round of applause after another. Jordan and Bess brought the crowd to their feet. Even Carlos took a bow, to the cheers of the cast and crew.

When the accolades were finally over, Carlos brought all of the players together backstage. "People, you were incredible!" he said as the stagehands slapped him on the back. "I am so proud of all of you. We did it!"

The cast and crew cheered again, and Nancy joined in with them. They'd come through a lot together these past few days. And although Nancy knew it wasn't over yet, it still felt right to celebrate their resounding success.

"Congratulations, everyone," Tim chimed in, shaking hands. "I was out there in the lobby just now, and it's official—they love the play."

Stella was close behind him. "I'd have to say

those firecrackers absolutely backfired on whoever set them," she said happily. "It's just going to be more great publicity for us. Carlos, we'll be able to extend this run forever if we want to!" She gave him a bear hug, and he returned it.

"Well, there'll be time to talk about that later," Carlos said. "Tonight we celebrate. Starting right here in thirty minutes!" That received the loudest cheer of all.

Nancy followed the others. She felt eager to get out of her costume and remove her stage makeup.

Bess was mobbed by the cast and crew on her way back to her dressing room. Nancy smiled. It was probably the biggest night of Bess's life; Nancy had never seen her friend look happier. But, inside, a prickle of worry stayed with Nancy. She knew that the worst yet could come—whoever was behind the sabotage and scare tactics seemed relentless.

Nancy entered the dressing room after Bess, closing the door behind her.

"Everything was perfect," Nancy told her friend. "You were fantastic! I knew you would be."

"Thanks," Bess said. "I have to admit those firecrackers really threw me."

"You stayed really calm," Nancy said. "Even if . . . hey, what's this?"

A white envelope had been slipped under the door. Nancy got up to retrieve it and saw Bess's name printed on the front. She handed it to her friend.

Bess opened the envelope, then burst out, "Listen to this, Nan: 'Congratulations to an incomparable leading lady—Yours, Jordan.' I can't believe it! He thinks I was good, doesn't he?" Bess's eyes sparkled with happiness.

"You're star quality, Bess Marvin," Nancy told her warmly.

"And you were born to play the role of Hayley Karr," Bess said. "You were great."

"I was pretty jittery, too," Nancy said. "I was sure those firecrackers were a gun." She hesitated for a second. "I don't want to alarm you, Bess," Nancy said finally. "But I think we have to stay alert. We still don't know who's behind all these pranks."

Bess agreed, and Nancy filled her in on what she'd found beneath the stage earlier that night.

"Poor Hugh," Bess said sympathetically. "I know Carlos thinks he's guilty, but I don't. I think he's just having rotten luck."

That matched Nancy's perception. Privately, she tried to figure out who could have set off the firecrackers at the back of the house. Hugh and Stella were the only people not on the stage. If Hugh had been telling the truth, the evidence pointed to Stella. The publicist certainly had a lot to gain from tonight's incident. The firecrackers would definitely generate more publicity for the show. Nancy resolved to ask Stella a few questions at the cast party.

Nancy got dressed in navy silk pants and a matching top. Bess had brought a filmy floral dress to change into. Together they returned to the stage, where everyone else was gathering.

The velvet front curtain was drawn across the front of the stage, and most of the furniture and props had been cleared from the stage area. In its place was a large buffet table laden with platters of sandwiches, chips, pretzels, and an enormous punch bowl with cups around it. The cast and crew surrounded the table, waiting their turn to fill their plates and glasses.

Nancy noticed Carlos standing to one side, beaming at the proceedings. With him was Stella, who was busily adding up figures on a tally sheet.

"Even better than I thought," Nancy heard her remark.

Jordan sat in the ornate desk chair from the set. He signed autographs for a few audience members who had wandered backstage to offer their congratulations.

"Hungry, Bess?" Nancy asked.

Bess nodded. "I'm starved."

As the girls filled their plates, they saw Carlos shaking hands with Kate Grenoble, who was all smiles, for once.

Bess froze. "Oh, no!" she whispered to Nancy. "Look at how happy Kate looks. Do you think Carlos is going to pull the part from me and give it to Kate?"

Nancy was puzzled. "Why would he do that? You've got an adoring audience."

"Because I'm not really a professional," Bess moaned.

"You're a professional now," Nancy said. "It's official."

As Nancy watched the pair, she remembered Jordan's explanation for the phone call. Had Kate found out about losing her TV role yet?

Kate was still beaming. Jordan came up behind her and said something that made her and Carlos laugh. Then Jordan gave Kate a sizzling kiss. Maybe Jordan made up that whole story, Nancy thought.

Bess sighed. "And there goes my fantasy," she said. "Tonight, when he kissed me, I could swear he really meant it. Could he be that good a fake, Nan?"

"He's an actor, Bess," Nancy reminded her soberly. "Actors are supposed to be convincing. And from what I could see tonight, he was, uh, extremely convincing."

"You can say that again," Bess said. "Anyway, I keep telling myself to enjoy it while it lasts—I still get to kiss him several times a night."

"That's the spirit," Nancy said, grinning. She didn't want to let on to Bess how worried she felt.

"Hey, Nan," Bess said suddenly. "Let's get pictures of everybody. Where's the camera?"

"In the trunk of my car," Nancy replied. "I'll get it, if you like."

"No, thanks, I'll go myself," Bess said. "Keys, please?"

Nancy handed her the keys, and Bess went out the backstage door to the parking lot behind the theater.

Nancy took a moment to survey the party guests. Jordan and Kate were gone. They sure made a quick exit, Nancy thought. Did they just want to be alone together? Or was there some other reason to make a quick getaway?

"It's so unfair!" On the love seat, Zoe Adams was holding court, telling anyone who would listen what she'd been through. Nancy could see her eyeing Carlos, probably waiting for the moment when she could pull him aside and demand her part back.

For the hundredth time that night, Nancy realized that the danger wasn't over. Not by a long shot.

Suddenly she felt chilled, and not just by her dark thoughts. The air conditioning backstage was going full blast.

Nancy decided to go out to the car; she remembered having tossed a sweater into the backseat that morning. Bess would still be out there with the keys.

Nancy passed through the backstage door and out into the parking lot. She had parked her car at the far end of the lot, under the trees, where the sun wouldn't beat down on it all day.

She spotted the Mustang. But where was Bess? Nancy's eyes searched the parking lot, which was almost empty by now. The wind was blowing, and large droplets of rain had started to fall; it felt like the beginning of a storm.

Nancy heard a scraping noise from the far end of the parking lot. A hundred feet away, sheltered by the trees from the glare of the street lights, a masked figure dressed in black was wrestling with Bess!

"Help!" Bess screamed, lashing out at her attacker.

"Bess!" Nancy cried.

But before Nancy could move, the figure wrestled Bess into the front seat of a black car. Then he ducked into the car beside her, and revved the motor.

Nancy rushed for the car, but it was too late. With a screeching of brakes, the driver backed up, then sped past the gates of the parking lot, turning up gravel in the car's wake.

There was a crash of thunder, and then the rain began to stream down. Nancy tried to make out the license plate of the speeding car, but it was a blur.

As she stood in the pouring rain, cold fear gripped Nancy. Bess had been kidnapped, and Nancy had no idea where she'd been taken.

Chapter Twelve

DESPERATELY, NANCY RAN for her car. Then she remembered: Bess had her keys!

Nancy scanned the street for a taxi but couldn't find one. Besides, now that it was raining, everyone would be clamoring for cabs. She dashed to the theater's back door: She'd try to borrow a car from someone inside the theater.

As she ran, she thought frantically of the anonymous kidnapper. He was dressed in black, like Jordan, but he'd been wearing the stolen cat-burglar costume. Could it have been Jordan? Had the actor made up the whole story about the missing costume?

As Nancy reached for the door, it opened. "Didn't mean to scare you," Hugh said.

"I need a car—fast," Nancy blurted out. If anyone would be willing to help, she felt it would be Hugh. Unless he was somehow connected with the abduction. But that was a chance she was going to have to take.

"Bess has been kidnapped." The words stumbled out.

"What?" Hugh began. Then he seemed to realize the urgency of the situation. "We can take my car," he said, pulling Nancy quickly toward the parking lot.

Nancy followed him across the dimly lit lot, mentally planning the route she would take to look for Bess. She hadn't been able to get the car's license plate, but maybe she'd recognize the model.

Hugh fumbled for his keys, unlocked the passenger side of his compact car, and let her in.

Hugh turned over the engine, which sputtered and died. "C'mon, c'mon," he said, pumping his foot on the gas pedal impatiently.

Suddenly, Nancy felt panic. Why was Hugh about to leave the theater when she ran inside? Hugh himself hadn't abducted Bess, but that didn't mean he wasn't somehow involved. If he wanted to, Nancy realized, he could flood the engine of his car so it wouldn't start. The sabotage could be that simple.

Nancy watched Hugh try to start the car twice more before she decided to bolt. "Thanks for trying," she said. "I'd better go call the police."

"I'm sorry, Nancy," Hugh mumbled. "I let you down."

"It's okay. I know you tried to help Bess," she told him, then she dashed into the theater.

Nancy raced through the backstage hallways until she reached the pay phone outside the dressing room. She dialed the police and gave her report as quickly as she could; the police replied that they were on their way. Then Nancy hurried back to the cast party. Maybe she could question some of the cast members while she waited for the police.

Carlos spotted her right away. "You didn't get your sweater?" He put his arm around Nancy's shoulders and handed her a glass of punch.

"I'm not chilly after all," she said, moving away from him. She quickly scanned the room, taking in the party guests.

"When did Jordan and Kate leave the

party—when did you last see them?" she questioned Carlos.

"Just a few minutes before you went out to the car," Carlos answered. "Where's Bess, anyway? I want us all to drink a toast to her."

Nancy hesitated. Then, not knowing what else to do, she whispered the news of Bess's abduction to the director. She watched his face to see his reaction.

"What a nightmare!" Carlos exploded in a hoarse whisper. "And what terrible timing," he added. "Have you called the police?"

"They're on their way," Nancy assured him.

"I've got to call Stella," Carlos said. "And I should let the whole cast know what's going on." Carlos mounted a chair and clinked his glass with a fork to get everyone's attention. After making the announcement, he disappeared into the office to make his phone call.

He's certainly upset, Nancy thought, but for the wrong reasons! All he seemed to care about was publicity for the show. And where was Stella anyway? It was opening night—she was supposed to be at the party.

Just then, Jordan walked in with Kate on his arm. Nancy glanced at her watch: It had been thirty-five minutes since Bess was abducted—just enough time for Jordan and Kate to deposit her somewhere and return to the party.

Nancy turned to greet them both at the door and to tell them about Bess before anyone else did. "Hi," she said as casually as she could manage. "What've you two been up to?"

Kate thrust her hand out to Nancy, displaying a flashy diamond ring. "Jordan and I are engaged," she said gleefully. "He spirited me away to propose and we just *had* to come back to tell everyone!"

Nancy told them about the kidnapping, looking from Jordan to Kate to see their expressions. She noticed that Jordan's hair was tousled and that he had lipstick on his collar. Were these signs of passion—or tricks to make the couple's story about being engaged more plausible?

"Poor Bess!" Kate exclaimed. She looked at Jordan. He also looked concerned, Nancy noted. But before he could answer, Kate went on. "If Bess isn't around, you'll need someone to go on tomorrow night." Her tone was matter-of-fact. "And Zoe's out of the question—so it'll have to be me."

"Kate, really." Jordan took his fiancée's arm, then turned to Nancy. "This is terrible news," he said. "You must be really worried. Is there anything we can do?"

"The police are on their way," Nancy informed him. "If you'll excuse me, I've got business to take care of." Nancy had found out all she could for now.

Nancy moved on to Zoe, who was sitting in the corner of the room. She pulled up a chair and joined them.

"You're in too much pain," Carlos was saying.

"I'm not!" Zoe insisted. "And anyway, I can outdo Bess any day—sling or no sling."

Carlos threw up his arms in frustration. "I refuse to talk about this further. Not while poor Bess is missing," he said. "Ah, the police are here." He jumped to his feet and hurried over to the officers.

Relief flooded over Nancy. Help had arrived. But half an hour later, her hopes had dimmed. The police questioned everyone, but they, like Nancy, didn't have any real leads. As he left, Officer Streithorst promised to stay in touch with Nancy.

By midnight the crowd had thinned. Nancy slumped in a chair, desperately hoping that Bess was okay. Carlos approached her, his brow furrowed. "Isn't it too late for you to go back to River Heights?"

"I'm staying at the hotel around the corner," Nancy lied quickly. Maybe she could come back later to search the theater without Carlos's knowing.

"So long, see you tomorrow," Kate and Jordan called. They were the last to leave, and Nancy found herself alone with Carlos.

The director waved goodbye to the couple and turned his attention to Nancy. He took her arm and steered her toward his office. He sank down onto the worn sofa beside his desk. Nancy sat as well, folding her legs beneath her and facing Carlos.

"I know I reacted rather callously out there," Carlos said.

Nancy looked at him questioningly.

"I wish I had taken the accidents around here more seriously. Maybe if I had, Bess would be—"

Carlos stopped short. Nancy felt her eyes well up. "It's just that I've had this play on my mind for so long—I almost couldn't think of anything else," Carlos went on.

He did look exhausted, Nancy noticed. She remembered how he'd reacted to the news about Bess by mentioning Stella. "By the way, where was Stella tonight?" she asked.

"She's at home—she's got some kind of bug," Carlos said.

"Wasn't she disappointed about missing opening night?" Nancy probed.

"Of course," Carlos said. "She's been looking forward to this for almost a year—we all have. . . ." His voice faltered, and he cleared his throat.

Nancy glanced at the wall clock. Soon it would be too late to do any serious investigating. "I'm afraid I've got to get back to the hotel," she said, getting up from the couch.

"It's late. I'll walk you there," Carlos said.

"Thanks, but no," Nancy said. And with that she closed the door firmly behind her.

Outside, it was still raining lightly, but Nancy didn't care. She needed to clear her head—to walk and to think.

Just as she began hurrying down the street, she stopped short: It was already much later than the time she'd told her father and Hannah to expect her home. If she didn't call, they would be frantic. She darted into Rick's Café to find a phone.

Rick's was still abuzz with people. This place is *always* packed, Nancy thought, as she waited on line to use the telephone. Her mind flashed again to the image of Bess being forced into the car.

Who had kidnapped Bess and why? In a way, Nancy had too many suspects—she had to narrow down her list.

First, there were Carlos and Stella; both seemed desperate to make the play a success. Stella had been missing from the party tonight; she could have been the one to grab Bess.

But wouldn't Carlos be satisfied with the publicity they'd already gotten? Nancy thought a moment later. After all, opening night had been a smash.

Zoe and Kate were more likely suspects. But Nancy had to admit that both women were pretty open about wanting the role of Xena. If either one was guilty, wouldn't she have tried to camouflage how much she wanted to play the lead? And if it were Kate, where did Jordan fit in?

As for Hugh . . . Nancy wasn't sure. Suddenly, she found herself wishing she'd told the police about his conveniently stalled car and his living quarters in the theater. Maybe he'd been duping Nancy all along.

Nancy tapped her foot impatiently. The phone was still being used. As she gazed around the walls, she noticed a framed article proclaiming Rick's Café as the city's hottest new spot in the neighborhood. "A Café Worth the Wait," the headline read. Nancy quickly skimmed the text, which described the café's great food and fabulous location—in the heart of one of Chicago's newly trendy neighborhoods. It was an area best known, according to the article, for its shopping, hot nightspots, and "skyrocketing real estate values."

Nancy stopped cold. She'd missed something obvious and limited her suspects to people directly connected to the Remington Theater. Perhaps she had overlooked someone else—someone who wanted the theater to fail so that he could succeed.

She spun around and stopped the first waiter she could find.

"Is Rick here tonight?" she asked. The waiter directed her to a dark booth in the back of the restaurant.

Rick sat alone, wearing a white dinner jacket and sipping a drink.

Nancy sat down opposite him. "Business sure is booming," she began.

"Sure is," he agreed. "In fact, in the six months since we've been here, I haven't had more than a handful of slow nights."

"The neighborhood's really in now—I'll bet you pay an awful lot of rent for this place."

"You said it," Rick answered openly. "And it looks like it will more than double once we take over the space next door."

"What?" Nancy stared at him, feeling the color drain from her face. "You're taking over the space next door? You mean the Remington Theater?"

Rick nodded. "Didn't you hear? Tim says that Carlos is eager to move the play as soon as he can. That production has been plagued with accidents since rehearsals began. Carlos can't wait to get out of there."

Nancy's blood ran cold. Her hunch was right. "Thanks for the info," Nancy said to Rick, jumping to her feet. She sped to the phone, ready to call her dad and contact the police again. But the line was even longer than before, so she dashed out into the rainy night to find a pay phone.

Nancy turned right, heading for the corner. Then a car pulled up alongside her at the curb.

"Nancy," the driver called, "can I offer you a ride?"

Her heart pounding, Nancy stooped to see the speaker's face.

Behind the wheel of the black car, a figure was dressed in Jordan's dark cat-burglar costume. Nancy knew who he was even before he pulled off the mask to reveal his face.

It was Tim Talcott.

Chapter Thirteen

NANCY TURNED and started racing back toward Rick's. But Tim was too fast for her. He jumped out of the car, grabbed her arm, and twisted it painfully behind her back. She opened her mouth to scream, but Tim murmured a warning in her ear: "You scream and you'll never see Bess again."

Nancy snapped her mouth shut, and Tim led her back to the car.

"Get in," he said brusquely, pushing her into the passenger seat.

Nancy's mind was racing. The whole thing made sense now. He could probably get three or four times more rent from Rick than from Carlos and his father. But he couldn't throw his tenants out—Carlos said they had a long-term lease. But if they left because too many accidents were happening . . .

"You should have kept your nose out of things," Tim growled.

Nancy ignored the comment.

"Where are we going?" she asked.

"You know very well where we're going," Tim snapped. "You're about to join Bess." He drove to the corner and made a left, away from the theater. He maneuvered the car with one hand, using a special knob attached to the steering wheel to make the turn.

"What a convenient gadget," Nancy said, pointing to the knob to distract him.

"It leaves one hand free to keep nosy girls from getting out of hand," he snarled.

Nancy kept quiet. As long as Tim didn't blindfold her, she'd soon know Bess's location.

"Where are we going?" she ventured again.

"Where do you think?" he said tensely. "It's the last place anyone would look—the theater. But we're gonna wait and make sure that moron Carlos doesn't see us."

Now Nancy had what she needed: a location. Tim reached the next intersection and braked. Nancy held her breath, waiting for the car to come to a stop. Then, as she saw a car approach from the opposite direction, she shouted, "Tim—watch out!"

On reflex, Tim grabbed the wheel with both hands. In that split second, Nancy grabbed the door handle. She threw herself out of the car and rolled onto the street.

She heard the car brakes screech and Tim's voice call out her name. She tried to get to her feet, but she felt a searing pain in her right ankle. She fell back to the ground. In an instant, Tim was standing over her.

"You're even less trustworthy than I thought," he growled, "and that means no second chances." Tim yanked Nancy to her feet and dragged her limping to the car.

"Get in," he said, then slammed the door after her. He reached into the backseat for a roll of duct tape. After tearing off several pieces with his teeth, he pulled a rag from the glove compartment and stuffed it in Nancy's mouth, then sealed it with the tape. Next he wound a length of tape around Nancy's wrists, binding them together behind her back.

Don't panic, Nancy told herself. *It's not over yet*. But her hopes were fading fast—how would she ever get out of this one? Dimly, she realized she'd never called her father and

Hannah. If only there were some way for them to come to her rescue.

Tim drove aimlessly for what felt like at least twenty minutes. Finally, he pulled up into the dark lot behind the theater and parked just outside the rear stage door. He opened the car door and jerked Nancy to her feet. Then he pushed her in front of him toward the stage door and unlocked it.

Roughly, Tim pulled Nancy through the theater's back hallways, stopping abruptly to produce a key to an entrance Nancy had never seen before. She tried hard not to show surprise, breathing as evenly as she could and keeping her face expressionless.

Behind the door lay a stairwell that led down two flights to a subbasement. Tim led her to the bottom, where Nancy could see a labyrinth of passageways branching out in all directions.

Nancy knew that this was a level lower than the one she had explored. She wondered if anyone else even knew of its existence. After all, Tim was probably the only person with an actual floor plan of the place.

Tim pulled Nancy along, weaving from side to side like a subway car along a serpentine railway. A single bare lightbulb punctuated each passage. Tim stopped abruptly and Nancy bumped into him.

"Don't try anything," he warned. Nancy narrowed her eyes in silent protest. They faced another door, this one made of metal. Tim grabbed the ring of keys at his waist and seized a skeleton key, opening the door.

Nancy was met by total darkness and a series of muffled grunts. Was it Bess? If it was, she had obviously been gagged, too.

Tim flicked on the overhead light to reveal Bess seated in a wooden chair. Black tape covered her mouth, and her hands were tied behind her back.

"Nancy Drew, meet your costar in this drama, Bess Marvin," Tim said sarcastically. Nancy could see the look of terror in her friend's eyes.

Tim grabbed another chair and placed it beside Bess. "Sit down," he commanded Nancy, forcing her into the seat and tying her up. "Now that I've finally got the two of you in one place, I can relax a little." When he finished, he stood back and gazed at the two girls; Nancy could see he was savoring his triumph.

Tim began pacing in front of Nancy and Bess, as if he were giving a performance.

"So much for opening night," he said harshly. "Looks like it's curtains for both of you *and* the theater. Not that it was a bad idea when I bought the place two years ago. I paid next to nothing for the property," he boasted, "and a theater made the neighborhood more artsy—more in demand. My one mistake was giving those clowns a five-year lease. I didn't realize how fast the neighborhood would change."

Tim began pacing more furiously. "Timing is everything in this business, next to location. Rick is ready to expand right now, and he can already afford five times what these lightweights are paying." Tim paused to glare at Nancy and Bess. "The plan was going fine, until the two of you showed up and started nosing around," he added, glancing at Nancy.

"But all of that is about to be taken care of. I'll just get rid of you—and pin it on everyone's favorite scapegoat, Hugh."

At the mention of Hugh, Nancy's mind raced. Did Tim know that Hugh was living in the building?

"I'd love to hear your applause for my clever plot," Tim went on, "but I'll wait until the very end, after I've ditched my car and every other trace of evidence."

He moved toward the door. "And just so you know I've got a heart, I'll leave the light on so you don't get scared," he sneered. With that, he slammed the door behind him. Nancy heard his footsteps become fainter and fainter down the corridor. Nancy and Bess exchanged desperate glances.

Nancy cast her eyes around the room. They were in some kind of supply room, with unpainted plasterboard walls. The only possible hope Nancy saw was a small closet, with its door slightly ajar.

Nancy threw all of her weight forward, and stood up, her hands still tied to the chair. She winced at the pain in her ankle, which she knew must be swollen. Awkwardly, she managed to hop over to the closet.

Watching from the sidelines, Bess murmured as if to cheer Nancy on. In one swift gesture, Nancy flung open the door with her elbow and revealed the closet's disappointing contents: bottles of cleaning supplies piled in a rusty wire grocery cart, and a mop.

Bess let out a cry, and Nancy understood her desperation. But she had an idea. Lowering her chin to the cart, she tipped it over and let the contents spill onto the concrete floor, knocking over the mop in the process. Then she sat back down on the chair. It was a desperate plan, but Nancy was out of other ideas.

Gripping the mop handle between her feet, she began to tap out the SOS signal. From his comment to Nancy during the dress rehearsal, Nancy was pretty sure that Hugh knew the SOS signal. She only hoped he was near enough to hear it. She did it over and over again.

When Nancy glanced back at Bess, her friend looked puzzled. Nancy crinkled her eyes, trying to give Bess a hopeful smile.

A short while later, Nancy and Bess heard pounding at the door. "Open up!" the voice demanded. Nancy shoved her chair back, away from the door, using her eyes and head to get Bess to follow her example. If the person outside broke down the door, she and Bess would need to stay clear of his path.

As if on cue, the door burst open. Hugh barreled into the room, smashing into the grocery cart and collapsing on the floor.

"What the—?" Hugh looked as if he couldn't believe what he saw. He leaped to his feet and went to Bess. Slowly, he eased the tape from her mouth, then removed the rag.

"Find Tim," Bess blurted as soon as she was

able. "He did it—everything—kidnapped me—and Nancy. And you've got to—"

"Are you all right?" Hugh cut in.

"Yes," Bess admitted. "Untie us and let's get out of here!"

Hugh quickly untied the girls, and they hurried through the passages to the rear of the building.

Just as they reached the stairs, a male voice echoed through the corridor. "Hold it right there."

Bess gasped, and Nancy whirled around. Once again, Tim had them trapped, and this time he was brandishing a revolver.

Chapter Fourteen

"I HAD A HUNCH I'd left some business unfinished," Tim said menacingly. He was out of breath and panting hard. "How did you find the leading lady and her friend, Hugh?" Tim asked.

"Give it up, Tim," Hugh shot back. "You'll throw away your whole life if you hurt me or those girls."

In the pale glow of the exterior light, Nancy saw that Tim's clothing was wet. He must have hidden his car, then raced back here, she reasoned.

"I'll do whatever I want," Tim snapped. "It's too bad for you that you wandered into this scene." He let out a vicious laugh. "Because this one ends with a bang." Slowly, he released the safety catch on the gun.

Nancy's heart sank at the ominous clicking sound. She looked fleetingly at Bess and then at Hugh. Their only hope was Bess, who stood closest to the brick wall, where a fire alarm was mounted.

"I don't think Hugh knows your master plan," Nancy told Tim, playing for time. If only she could get Bess to focus on the fire alarm on the brick wall behind her. "He didn't know you were trying to drive out Carlos to rent out the property to Rick."

"Hugh doesn't give a hoot about real estate," Tim spat. "All he cares about is his precious play—and Bess." He mocked Hugh with false sympathy. "Poor Hugh. In love with the leading lady—who's in love with the leading man."

Nancy took advantage of Tim's inattention. As he spoke, she lifted her eyes the slightest bit, gazing deliberately past Bess, fixing her eyes on the small rectangular fire box behind her on the wall. If only Bess would pick up the signal!

"I've waited two long years for this moment," Tim sneered, keeping his eyes on Hugh. "I've watched you bumble around—

none of you theater types has any business sense." He faced Nancy abruptly. "And I had *you* figured out as soon as I met you—you're nothing but an amateur."

Nancy stood stock-still and kept her expression perfectly neutral.

"Listen, Tim," Hugh reasoned, "if your beef's with me, then why don't you just take care of me. You can think of another way to make Bess and Nancy disappear—they're harmless."

"Nice try," Tim said. "But you're a dead man, and so are your friends here." Tim extended the gun closer to them.

Nancy gritted her teeth. So far, Bess hadn't picked up her cues at all. But maybe Nancy could try something else. . . .

Tim turned his attention to Bess, who stared at him defiantly. "And you—" he said. "You were so worried about playing with the big kids that you didn't even get it. Jordan McCabe wouldn't look at you in a million years."

"Wait just a minute," Bess began. Nancy didn't hear the rest as she sprang into action. She took aim at Tim, and in one seamless movement, she kicked the weapon out of his hand. He let out a cry.

"The gun!" Bess shouted.

Nancy followed the revolver's trajectory. She watched, satisfied, as Hugh lunged for it and caught the handle.

Nancy raced over to the brick wall. She smashed the glass of the fire alarm, letting loose a shrill ringing sound that pierced the night. Hugh kept the gun trained on Tim.

Bess let out a cry of relief. Tim's eyes were wide with astonishment. "The fire department will be here any minute," Nancy announced.

"Good work, Drew," Bess said. "Both of you," she added as she turned to smile at Hugh. Then she glanced back at Tim. "Tough break. I guess you were outdone by us *amateurs*—isn't that what you called us?"

"Why don't you tell us how you made all those accidents happen?" Nancy prodded Tim. "Starting with the problem with the sofa and the water damage to the costumes."

Tim shrugged. He was outnumbered, and he knew it. "Well, I never meant to hurt anybody in the beginning," he said slowly. "I just hoped Carlos would want to back out of the lease." He paused. "The first couple of accidents were easy—I just hung around, and when no one was looking, I doused the costumes with water and made it look like the sprinkler system had gone off randomly. I wanted it to look like the building was falling apart so that you guys would *have* to find another space."

"But Carlos didn't want to move," Nancy said. "He wanted to stay here. Is that why you ruined the sofa?"

Tim nodded. "That was just a prank to make Hugh look bad. Once Carlos started blaming Hugh, he was an easy target. I fooled with the springs of the love seat until it gave way when McCabe sat on it."

Nancy nodded. "What about the stage-door banister?" she asked.

"That was a good one," Tim boasted. "The fire, too. I was the one who found it—and the one who started it."

"What about the blanks in the gun?" Nancy asked.

"You already know what I'm going to say," Tim said contemptuously. "I emptied the blanks and replaced them with live ammunition. I never meant for anyone to get shot. Jordan was supposed to be aiming at the portrait—not at Zoe."

"How about the ruined head shot of me?" Bess asked.

"That was no big deal," Tim told her. "I just

pulled it from the display and smeared it up a little. Hanging around the theater has taught me a few tricks. Then I had my secretary drive the package out to River Heights. I was just trying to scare you."

"You managed to do that, all right," Bess said under her breath.

Nancy pressed on. "The bookcase falling—how did that accident happen?"

Tim scowled at Nancy. "I was controlling the whole thing from behind. At that point I was getting desperate!" Tim sighed. "I had no idea the accidents were going to sell tickets. And I was counting on Bess to be so lousy in the role of Xena that the production would close on opening night. But she was too good. She even knew how to sew costumes," he said, glaring at Bess.

Nancy noticed the satisfied grin on Bess's face.

"So I had to try to get rid of her," Tim continued, "and she made it easy for me to get hold of you, too."

The sound of nearby sirens put an end to the conversation. The fire department arrived first, surrounding and detaining Tim until the police showed up and cuffed him.

As they led Tim down the corridor in handcuffs, Nancy heaved a sigh of relief. "It's finally curtains for him," she told Bess. Then she hobbled off on her swollen ankle to find a phone to let her father know she was okay.

For the first time since rehearsals began, the Remington Theater felt safe and comfortable to Nancy. Zoe and Kate were nowhere to be seen. Bess was comfortable in her new role. Nancy was even starting to enjoy playing the maid.

Carlos sat center stage, in the drawing room's desk chair. "It just never crossed my mind that Tim could have been the one causing all these accidents." He shook his head woefully. "But I can tell you this, Hugh," he went on, "I'm sorry I misjudged you. May I respectfully request that you rejoin the Remington Theater?"

Hugh and Bess sat together on the love seat. Hugh answered, "You mean I can have my old job back?" His voice was cautious.

"You can have your old job back," Carlos confirmed. "If you still want it, that is."

Hugh glanced at Bess. "It kind of depends," he said quietly. "I might be too distracted to do a good job."

Bess blushed and took Hugh's hand. "Don't

worry," she reassured him, "we can make time to see each other before the show—and after!"

"Are you serious?" Hugh asked.

"I'm not acting," Bess said with a twinkle in her eye.

"One thing, though," Nancy cut in. "If you're back in the production, you'll need a real place to live." She looked at Carlos.

Carlos cleared his throat. "You would actually be doing me a favor if you'd have a talk with a friend of mine. He's looking for a roommate and having a hard time finding just the right guy. You see, he's a writer, and he needs someone who's extremely quiet." He smiled at Hugh.

"That would be me," Hugh said shyly.

"It's totally perfect!" Bess exclaimed. "Two writers teaming up!" She kissed Hugh impulsively on the cheek.

"So you two will be rehearsing together, again," Nancy said, trying to keep the smile from her face. "And not just for *Mystery Loves Company.*"

Bess looked at her quizzically. "What are you talking about, Nan? Of course we'll be rehearsing for the play—what else is there?"

Nancy's eyes twinkled. "From the look of

things, you'll be rehearsing for romance, too!" she joked.

Bess groaned and so did Hugh.

"Very funny," Bess said.

"Do me a favor, Nancy," Carlos spoke up. "Stick to drama, okay? Comedy is clearly *not* your thing."

"You have my word," the detective vowed. Then she took her spot behind the curtain.

Nancy's next case:

Nancy and George have gone undercover at Brookline High to make sure no more harm comes to track star Samantha Matero. A suspicious accident during a recent practice run resulted in a nasty ankle sprain. Now Samantha has received a series of threatening notes and phone calls, including the message "This time your ankle, next time your neck." Nancy discovers that the Brookline High track team is running on deception, blackmail, and intimidation. And while the constant attention and good looks of fellow student Paul Johnson nearly sidetrack her investigation, Nancy is determined to run this race to the end—before Samantha's hopes run out . . . in *Running into Trouble,* Case #115 in The Nancy Drew Files™.